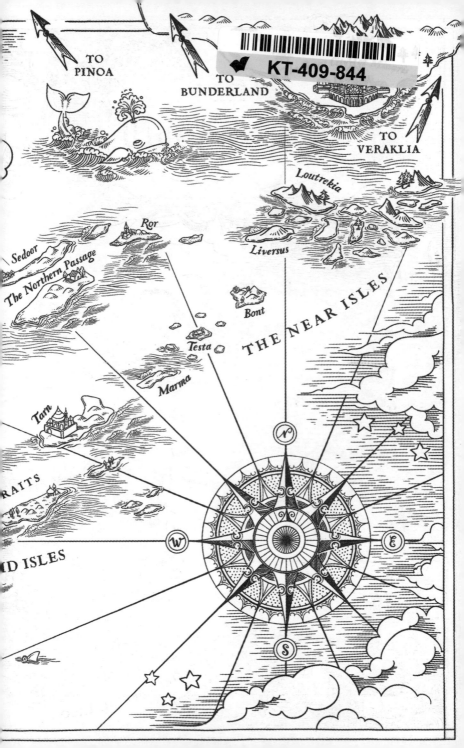

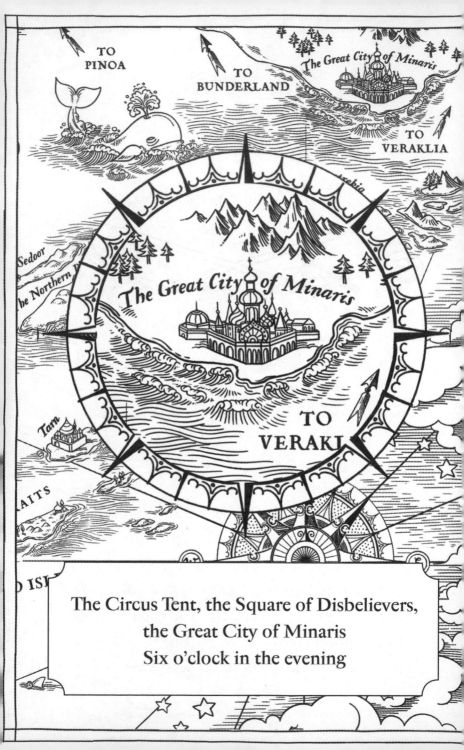

The Circus Tent, the Square of Disbelievers,
the Great City of Minaris
Six o'clock in the evening

THE
COMPANY
·OF·
EIGHT

·HARRIET·
WHITEHORN

Stripes

THE
LONGEST WORLD

THE FAR ISLES

Parma

Consta

SOUTHERN ARCHIPELAGO

Villuvia

Samay

The Island of Women

THE AVENI

Tali

Lection

TH

KATIRAN ARCHIPELAGO

I

A Star Over Your Head

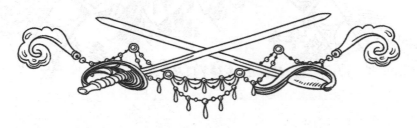

The girls were late.

They tore across the Square of Seas, their skates cutting into the thick ice that covered the city.

"This way is quickest!" Cass cried, grabbing her friend Tig's hand and pulling her down Truelove's Way.

They were headed for the Square of Disbelievers where the giant blue Circus tent had stood for five glorious days. That night was the Grand Finale and Cass had queued for hours and paid a good many silvers for two tickets. And then Mrs Potts had deliberately made them late by giving Tig too much work to do, or at least that's what it

1

seemed like to Cass.

The clocks struck six as the girls sped along Tick Alley, right at the centre of the watchmaking district. Cass shoved her fingers in her ears to shut out the deafening noise as they swerved into one of the narrow courts that led down to the Square of Disbelievers.

Everyone had already taken their seats, so the huge square was deserted. If the girls had been in less of a hurry they might have noticed how beautiful it looked, the whale-like tent glowing deep blue from the lights inside, casting everything else in the square into deep-violet and navy-blue shadow, except for the faint glimmer of the palace's silver domes. But they had no time to look around, hurtling themselves at the entrance and sliding the blades out from the bottom of their boots.

One of the circusters, as the stagehands were known, stood at the door, fabulously dressed in a red and gold outfit, his features hidden by a mask. He took their tickets and whispered that they would have to wait to take their seats because the show was about to begin. And sure enough, a moment later, the tent was plunged into complete darkness. Everyone instantly fell silent, anticipation shivering through the air.

Cass felt prickles of excitement as she heard the Circus Master, whose name was Ravellous, cry, "Welcome, one and all, to my domain – the Greatest Circus in the Longest World. Prepare to be amazed." His deep voice, magnified by a loud hailer, thundered around the tent.

Cass watched spellbound as, high above the audience, right at the very top of the tent, a single candle flame appeared. And then came a voice – a perfectly clear woman's voice – singing a sad but beautiful lament.

The light began to move slowly down towards the audience as if suspended in the air and then shifted to illuminate a face, lit up like a lovely singing ghost, descending down from the sky. She was Helene, the star of the show and Cass's heroine.

The rest of the company, dressed in dark cloaks and holding candles, walked out slowly into the arena, their voices joining with hers until the whole tent was filled with glorious, melancholy singing. They formed a ring facing the audience and as Helene reached the ground, they placed their candles on the floor and bowed solemnly.

The crowd erupted into applause and the music changed tempo to a fast beat as the performers threw off their cloaks to reveal bright, glittering costumes. The stagehands lit the arena torches and the lamps, brilliantly illuminating the tent. Trapezes were dropped and the acrobats divided; some stayed on the ground to form a human pyramid, while others leaped on to the trapezes, which were then raised and a breathtaking aerial show began.

Cass, along with the rest of the audience, was left dizzy with trying to watch so many different things at the same time.

"Just think, that will be you after tomorrow!" Tig whispered. "Cassandra Malvino, Star of the Circus!"

Cass made a face.

"Please don't jinx it," she whispered back.

"Sorry," said Tig. "But you're easily good enough. What time is your audition?"

"Noon," Cass replied, her stomach flipping with

nerves. Never in her life had she wanted anything as much. Except perhaps to bring her parents back from the dead. But since that was impossible, she had focused on merely the incredibly difficult.

Cass's father had been a famous acrobat, and Cass had inherited much of his natural grace and agility. But she also practised very, very hard.

Her guardian, Mrs Potts, thoroughly disapproved of acrobatics, considering them extremely unladylike, and thought that Circus people were "a bunch of bohemian hoodlums". So Cass practised in secret, up in the dusty attic of the Mansion of Fortune, the tatty old house where they lived, or out on the roof in the summer, with only an old book of her father's for instruction. Its title, written in curly gold lettering, was *Dr Bromver's Complete Guide to Acrobatics and Gymnastics*. Tig helped Cass, warning her if Mrs Potts ever looked like making one of her very rare trips up all those stairs.

When Mrs Potts had adopted Cass, after a fire had tragically killed her parents, Cass had been a pretty blond-haired moppet of seven and both had been genuinely fond of each other. Mrs Potts owned and ran the magical establishment in which Cass's mother, one of the foremost fortune tellers of her day, had worked and so Cass was used to visiting the house and being spoiled by the old lady. And the spoiling continued in the form of silk dresses and sweets, until it became clear, a couple of years before, when Cass was twelve, that she showed no magical ability at all – in fact the opposite. All her mother's skill had reversed, making Cass something known as an "obtuse", which was a person particularly insensitive to magic.

Some called it a gift in itself but for Mrs Potts it was a bitter blow – she had hoped to make a good amount of silvers out of Cass. The old lady had failed to hide her disappointment, leaving Cass angry and hurt. The pair had had an uneasy relationship ever since.

Cass had left Mrs Papworth's Academy for Young Ladies a couple of months before and Mrs Potts, still slightly resentful, was now determined that Cass should become something genteel that she could boast to her friends about, like a governess or draper's model. But Cass was simply not cut out for such a career – she had a restless energy that could not be contained and a desire for freedom that would not be dampened. For her, life on board the Circus Boat, not only working as an acrobat but also exploring the Islands, was as close to perfection as she could imagine.

"You may take your seats now," the circuster said when there was a moment's lull in the show and, after glancing at the tickets, directed them right to the front row of benches.

"These are amazing seats," Tig said.

"I know, I queued hours to get them," Cass replied.

As they sat down, Tig gasped and elbowed Cass, whispering, "Look who's over there!"

Cass followed her gaze and saw, sitting just to the front and side of them on a padded, throne-like chair, the object of Tig's undying love – Lord Enzo.

With his floppy blond hair and dark skin, he was instantly recognizable from the gossip sheets that Tig pored over when Mrs Potts hadn't got her scrubbing floors. Tig was a year or two older than Cass and always had a crush on someone.

Enzo's father, Lord Bastien, the Lord Protector of the Islands, sat next to him, and then on Enzo's other side, was a boy and girl who Cass didn't recognize. *Of course*, Cass thought fleetingly, *they must be in Minaris to celebrate King Lycus's engagement.* And then Cass's attention was drawn back to the show as the lights dimmed again and the trapeze artists began their daring display of aerial acrobatics.

There was a short interval in the middle of the performance when the audience stood up to stretch their legs and buy cones of shaved fruit ice and rum bonbons. Cass got a few coins out of her pocket – she didn't want Tig to spend any of the measly amount of silvers that Mrs Potts paid her – and bought a couple of pomegranate ice cones.

Cass was never entirely sure what happened next – did someone push her or perhaps she tripped? Anyway, something made her lurch forwards just as she was about to sit back down next to Tig, sending the ice cones catapulting out of her hands. One landed on the floor but the other flew into the air, turned upside down and tipped its chilly contents all over the boy who was now standing next to Enzo, making him yelp with the cold.

Enzo, Lord Bastien and the girl all burst out laughing and turned to see where the cone had come from.

"I'm so sorry," Cass cried, staring in horror at what she had done. She could hear, or rather *feel*, Tig vibrating with silent laughter beside her.

"I think someone is trying to get your attention, Rip," the girl said cattily.

The boy smiled as he wiped his face and rubbed his hands through his hair, shaking off the ice.

"It's fine," he said. "Really," he added, seeing Cass's mortified face.

"It's so hot in here, I wish someone would throw an ice cone over *me*," Lord Bastien drawled, puffing on a cigarillo.

"Well, this young lady appears to have the skills for the job," Enzo replied, laughing. "Perhaps if you ask her nicely she'll oblige?"

It was a remark that needed an amusing response, but poor Cass could think of nothing witty to say. She simply blushed and simpered and hated herself for it.

"Ignore them," the boy said kindly.

Cass was saved from any further embarrassment

by a loud drum roll signalling that the show was about to start again.

"I'm so sorry," she repeated as they all took their seats. She could feel her cheeks burning red.

"Couldn't you have thrown it over Lord Enzo instead?" Tig whispered to her. "Then I could have brushed the ice off him."

"Very funny," Cass whispered back, glad of the dark to hide her crimson face.

It didn't take long for Cass to be lost again in the excitement and spectacle of the Circus but as soon as it ended, her embarrassment returned and she grabbed Tig's hand and pulled her out of the tent so she didn't have to see any of Lord Bastien's party again.

Tig chattered about Lord Enzo all the way home – surely he was the best-looking boy in the whole world? Had Cass seen how green his eyes were? Did Cass think he had noticed her?

But Cass was barely listening, she was so focused on thinking through every move of her audition piece – was it bold and daring enough to impress Ravellous the Circus Master? she wondered nervously.

The Circus auditions were nearly as much of a spectacle as the Circus itself. They were always held down on the Great Quay of Thieves while the Circus tent was dismantled and the whole marvellous show was somehow crammed back on to the Circus Boat. It always reminded Cass of a children's pop-up book in reverse. Then the boat would sail off, cheered on by the crowd. It was part of the tradition that everyone auditioning would bring their bags, and usually their entire family, as they would have to leave there and then to sail around the Islands, not to return to Minaris for another year.

That afternoon Cass had carefully packed a large duffel bag with her clothes and most beloved possessions, and hidden it under her bed. Then, when Mrs Potts had popped out to the wine merchants, Cass had guiltily sneaked into her boudoir. She had taken a piece of Mrs Potts's finest writing paper, with the name of the mansion at the top, and using her best dipping pen had written a short note. It said:

*I, Emmelina Potts, happily give consent for my
ward, Cassandra Malvino, to join the Circus
and go with you to the Islands.
Signed Emmelina Potts*

Cass had used Mrs Potts's seal at the bottom of the note to make it as look as genuine as possible. She was usually a painstakingly honest person and felt bad about this act of deceit.

But since she was only fourteen, and therefore not in charge of her destiny for another whole year, she knew it was necessary for her glorious new life.

She decided that she would compose a letter of farewell to Mrs Potts the following morning, that Tig could give her if Cass passed the audition.

The Mansion of Fortune in the Square of Seas, where Cass lived with Mrs Potts, was at the centre of the magical district. This was the area where people who had no desire to go to bed at a reasonable hour flocked to. They would drink in the famous Inn of the Outraged Octopus or visit the magical establishments around the Square of Seas, where they could have their fortunes told, or their minds read, or try to trace long-lost relatives and friends through a form of telepathy called trancing.

It was sometimes hard to believe that magic had once been the most powerful force in the Longest World. It had all changed fifty or so years before when, exhausted by the bloodshed and horror of the final Magical War, the ordinary, non-magical people had risen up in revolt against the magicians and their petty quarrels. Almost all of the magicians were killed.

The few that survived either lived quietly in the magical districts of the great cities or fled to the remote, outer reaches of the Longest World, away from the prying eyes of the Magical Enforcers and their strictly imposed Laws of Magic, which allowed only very minor arts such as fortune telling or conjuring tricks to be practised.

As the girls skated under the Arch of Fate and back into the Square of Seas, a voice called, "Cass! Tig!" from above their heads.

They looked up to see their friend Lin leaning out of the window of her room in the Mansion of Truth. She was a few years older than both

Cass and Tig, and was something of a big sister to them. In the daytime, Lin looked rather like a beautiful boy, with her neat features and short hair, but at night she transformed herself with a wig and heavy make-up, to make sure she looked every bit the part of Minaris's most sought-after fortune teller. Cass felt Lin's green eyes sweep over her and her voice was light with excitement.

"You have a star over your head, Cass. It's faint because it's you but it's definitely there. Did something good happen today, something important?"

Tig burst out laughing. "Not unless you call chucking a load of ice over some poor boy good! But," she added, "he was with Lord Enzo. Perhaps your destiny is to marry Lord Enzo!"

Cass rolled her eyes. "I don't think so, but we have just been to the Circus." Lin knew all about the audition. "Do you think it's a good omen for tomorrow?"

"Maybe," Lin replied. A voice called from inside the room and she said, "Sorry but I must go. Good luck, Cass!"

The neighbouring Mansion of Fortune was buzzing with customers when they got back, and Mrs Potts greeted them with a martyred expression.

"Well, I hope you girls have had a lovely time," she said. "It's been a complete nightmare here without you and I have the most appalling headache."

Then she disappeared off into her room clutching a bottle of smelling salts and a large glass of Rimple's Finest, the strong Minarian liquor that she was so fond of.

The girls immediately got to work, running up and down stairs, escorting customers to the array of magicians and fortune tellers that Mrs Potts crammed into the mansion.

But a couple of hours later, as the square clock struck twelve, Tig caught Cass by the arm and said, "You go to bed – you need your energy for the audition tomorrow."

Cass thanked her friend and gratefully went to her room.

Every night before she climbed into bed, she had a ritual that she followed. The terrible fire that had killed her parents had also destroyed all their possessions except for a couple of objects that had been preserved in a small tin chest.

One was Dr Bromver's acrobatics book and the other was a small, framed picture that had belonged to Cass's mother. It was an oil painting of the Island of Women, which was where her mother, an orphan too, had grown up. Situated in the south-western archipelago of the Mid Isles, the small tropical island was famous not only for being a sanctuary for women but also an orphanage where unwanted babies were shipped to from all over the Longest World.

There was something about the vivid blues and lush dark greens of the picture that Cass loved and she found that however bad a day she had had, just a couple of moments looking at it soothed her. So every night, she would stand in front of it, and usually have a short conversation in her head with her parents and wish them good night.

That night her thoughts were entirely focused on the audition the following day.

"Please let Ravellous choose me tomorrow,

please please," she entreated them.

Cass felt as if she were leaning far out of a window, trying to grab something just out of reach. Her dream of being an acrobat was so near that she just needed to stretch a tiny bit further and it would be hers.

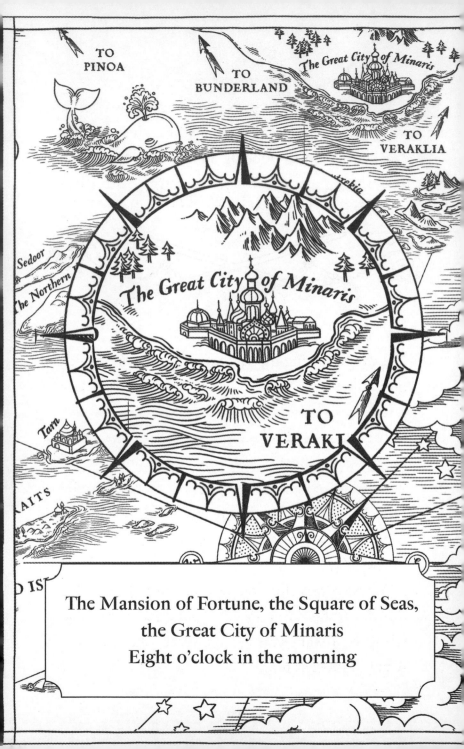

The Mansion of Fortune, the Square of Seas,
the Great City of Minaris
Eight o'clock in the morning

II

The Handkerchief

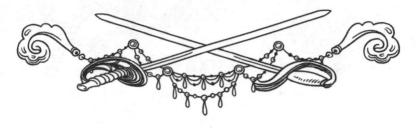

But the following morning, matters did not quite go to plan.

Cass woke early, and while the rest of the house was still asleep, she did her daily stretches, as instructed by Dr Bromver's book, then went downstairs to make some bitter tea. To her surprise she found Mrs Potts already up and about, with a fully painted face and dressed in her finest dark purple silk.

"I have a treat for you this morning, Cassandra dearest," she announced, sounding unusually friendly. "I want you to be in your blue silk and ready to leave at ten."

"Really?" Cass gave a start. The audition was at twelve. "Will the treat take long?" she asked carefully. She did not want to alert the old lady to anything.

"Oh no, not long at all," Mrs Potts replied. Cass weighed up whether to tell her she had an appointment at twelve and then decided against it. Mrs Potts loved to inject drama and mystery into everyday matters, so it was probably something as straightforward as taking Cass to one of the teahouses on the river for cacao and cake. That was her usual idea of a treat and would take no more than an hour so Cass would still have plenty of time to get to the audition.

"In the meantime," Mrs Potts went on, "I am off to Mr Magenta's to freshen up my curls." She patted her carrot-coloured locks and then added, "Why don't you come along and see if he can do anything with that hair of yours?"

Cass's hair was a constant bone of contention between them. It was a very thick and curly mop of messy, streaky blond that Cass was supposed to comb every day to stop it from tangling, but she rarely bothered. When she was young, in exasperation Mrs Potts had cut it short so it framed Cass's face like a mane, and her nickname at Mrs Papworth's Academy had been Lion. This dramatic hair was somewhat at odds with the rest of her face, which was rather peaceful with calm grey eyes and fair freckly skin.

"No thank you," Cass replied quickly. The last thing she wanted to do was sit still for an hour while Mr Magenta tugged and pulled and tutted at her hair.

"Very well," Mrs Potts replied tartly and bustled off.

Cass went upstairs to practise her routine and get dressed, layering her silk dress over the pantaloons and top that she wore for acrobatics, in case she had to go straight from the teahouse to the quay. She would be hot but it couldn't be helped.

Still thinking that she was off for tea and cake, Cass wasn't surprised to find a sledge and driver outside the house at ten, as Mrs Potts rarely skated anywhere. Once they had climbed in, it glided around the Square of Seas but instead of veering off towards the teahouses, it swung to the right, heading towards the City Gates.

"Where are we going?" Cass asked, alarmed. "I cannot be too long," she added.

Mrs Potts looked at her with a smug smile.

"You may change your mind when we get there," she said.

"No, really, Larina Nespov has invited me for luncheon," Cass lied, deliberately picking the richest of her old schoolmates.

"I'm sure you will be back in time," Mrs Potts replied with a dismissive smile, as the sledge trundled through the City Gates and out into the countryside beyond.

Spring was late that year, and the plains that surrounded the city were still covered in a thick snowy shroud that merged with the pale winter sky to form a vast expanse of dirty white. The only contrast in the scenery was the odd outcrop of trees, leafless black silhouettes at this time of year, and the clouds of starlings that rose and fell according to their whim. Some people might have found the landscape beautiful in its starkness but to Cass it was utterly depressing.

The sledge soon turned off the main road and passed through some grand iron gates.

"Why are we going to the Carpera Estate?" Cass asked with surprise as the mansion loomed up ahead of them. Cass had occasionally accompanied Mrs Potts and one of the fortune tellers there, when they had been summoned by the Carperas for readings.

"Because old Madame Carpera has asked to see you," Mrs Potts replied, suppressing a grin.

"But why?" Cass asked as the sledge drew up in front of the grand entrance portico.

"I have no idea," Mrs Potts lied. "Now straighten your dress and be sure to mind your manners," she said as the sledge came to a halt and a liveried servant appeared to help them down.

The house was just as Cass remembered it; huge, with so much chilly marble everywhere it felt like a bathhouse. They were ushered into a small room that, by contrast, was fiercely hot. Even though the day was dull, the blinds in the room were lowered and candles lit everywhere as if it were nighttime.

Mrs Potts advanced across the room, saying,

"Madame Carpera, what a delight to see you. May I introduce my ward, Cassandra, who I was telling you about."

Cass came forward and greeted the tiny figure wrapped up in layers of stiff silk. Time had faded and shrunk her features so much that only her watery blue eyes stood out of the folds of impossibly wrinkled skin.

After a moment's appraisal the old lady croaked, "Very good. Come and sit by me, Cassandra, so we may get better acquainted. I will just ring for some tea."

Cass did as she was told and sat on the velvet pouffe the old lady indicated, trying not to think about how hot she was getting.

The old lady asked her a few general questions about her time at Mrs Papworth's, until a tray with a large platter of chestnut macaroons and an old-fashioned silver tea service was brought in.

"Will you make the tea, Cassandra, please?" Madame Carpera asked. "Such a pleasure to see a young face at the tea trolley, don't you think, Mrs Potts?"

Cass groaned inwardly. The Minarian Tea

24

Ceremony was one of those things that Mrs Papworth had considered most important in a young lady's education. But somehow Cass had never got the hang of it, probably because she found it so incredibly dull. However, she didn't want to be rude, so she gamely set about measuring and mixing the tea, and swirling the teapot with hot water as the old ladies gossiped about the royal engagement. After letting it brew for a moment, Cass poured it into the delicate china cups and handed them round.

"Will you take a tot of Rimple's Finest in yours?" Madame Carpera asked Mrs Potts.

"Why not?" Mrs Potts said in a way that suggested that Rimple's was a rare treat.

"Very wise, in this cold weather," Madame Carpera remarked and passed her a silver flask, after she had sloshed a generous dash into her own tea. She then took a large slurp and grimaced. "You need practice with that, Cassandra," she said. Mrs Potts shot Cass a look, which she ignored and apologized amiably to the old lady.

The great brass clock on the mantelpiece struck eleven. *We should be going,* Cass thought, gulping down her tea. She turned to Mrs Potts, expecting that she would be thinking the same. But Mrs Potts was munching away on a macaroon, not looking like she wanted to go anywhere.

Cass was just wondering whether she should say something when Madame Carpera produced a snuffbox and noisily inhaled two large pinches of the orange powder. She offered it to Mrs Potts, who took it eagerly. Cass tried not to wince as the old ladies sniffed and snorted revoltingly, and then loudly blew their noses into their handkerchiefs. To distract herself, she stared up at the portrait above the chimney piece.

It was of a family group – a stern-looking man sat on a silk-covered sofa, glowering, with his richly dressed but dumpy wife beside him, and three young children grouped around them; an older boy and then two younger girls sitting on the floor. The smallest was clutching a toy lamb in her hand.

"Can you believe that is me?" Madame Carpera asked Cass. "Cuddling my little lamby," the old lady added in a baby voice.

Cass smiled politely in reply, as she felt to answer

either "yes" or "no" sounded vaguely rude.

"Look at your handsome brother! Even as a boy he was a heartbreaker," Mrs Potts exclaimed. "But I didn't know you had a sister."

"No, poor Liane," Madame Carpera said with a sigh. "Papa forbade us ever to speak of her after she left."

Mrs Potts face perked up, sensing gossip.

"Oh really?"

"It was a simply terrible business," Madame Carpera said, lowering her voice, as if the servants might be listening at the door. "Of course Liane was always the most appalling tomboy, scorning dresses and taking no interest in her appearance. And then, when she came of age, she refused to marry and went off to become a sword fighter, if you please. Have you ever heard of such a thing? A female sword fighter? The shock nearly killed Mama, I can tell you."

Cass thought it sounded rather marvellous but Mrs Potts made suitably disapproving noises and said, "Wasn't there one in the Magical Wars? Melia or something?"

"Yes, Mele, and it was her followers that Liane

went to join. The Company of something. Extremely peculiar," she said with a sniff. "Anyway, enough of the past, on to the future," she announced, turning her beady eyes back to Cass. "Now, my dear, I don't know how much Mrs Potts has told you about the post."

Cass couldn't keep the astonishment off her face.

"Nothing," Mrs Potts said delightedly. "I wanted it to be a wonderful surprise."

Post, what post? Cass thought with dread. *What in the Longest World has Mrs Potts been up to now?*

"Let me explain," Madame Carpera began. "I am looking for a companion. Someone young and lively, to keep me from feeling so old. You would spend the days sewing or reading to me, with just a few light duties such as dusting the ornaments, washing my underclothes, filling my snuffboxes and arranging my hair. In the winter we would stay indoors – I find a turn about the orangery quite sufficient fresh air and exercise. In the summer, if the weather is fine and not too sunny, I take a carriage out. As you can see the house is full of beautiful objects and books, enough to interest any young mind for a lifetime.

And of course every week my nephew comes for tea – that is the high point of my social calendar and I am sure it will be of yours."

Mrs Potts winked delightedly at Cass. But Cass was speechless with horrified amazement. How could Mrs Potts do this to her? To come and live with Madame Carpera would be like being buried alive in a marble tomb.

"You are somewhat rough around the edges, which can only be expected considering your background," Madame Carpera went on, making Mrs Potts's grin falter a little. "But with careful tuition that can be remedied. Finish your tea and I will show you the house and some of my treasures."

"That would be delightful," Mrs Potts said, as the clock struck eleven thirty.

But Cass had had enough.

"Thank you for the tea and the kind offer of the post, which I will definitely consider," she said, getting to her feet. "But I really must be getting back to Minaris now."

Madame Carpera looked distinctly irritated while Mrs Potts had a face like a pan of milk coming to the boil.

"But we haven't got to know each other yet," Madame Carpera complained. "Surely you can stay longer?" she appealed to Mrs Potts.

"Of course we can," Mrs Potts said with exaggerated politeness, while shooting Cass an evil look. "Perhaps you could show us some more of your family portraits?"

"What a splendid idea!" the old lady said. "And you must see my collection of ancient Minarian pottery too."

Cass knew that unless they left now she was going to be late. So, taking a deep breath, she said bravely, "No, I'm sorry but I really have to leave. As I told you –" she looked at Mrs Potts – "I'm expected at the Nespovs's at noon." *Please let this work*, she prayed. She felt as if the whole room was holding its breath.

"Nespov the merchant?" Madame Carpera queried and Cass nodded, hoping that the old lady was about to send them off with her blessing. "Oh, that's no problem at all. I will just get my secretary to send a messenger bird to their house, explaining that you have been detained with me. They'll quite understand." And she rang the bell.

Cass could have wept with exasperation as she listened to Madame Carpera giving the instructions. But what could she do? She couldn't possibly tell her the real reason she wanted to leave, so she had no option but to try to calm herself down by thinking that the Circus Boat would be there for hours and they would surely let her audition later that afternoon.

It was four o'clock by the time they finished. Cass had struggled to stop herself screaming in frustration at the old ladies and pelting them with the collection of priceless snuffboxes.

As Madame Carpera said goodbye, she instructed Mrs Potts, "So all is agreed then. I will send my carriage to fetch Cassandra tomorrow."

In the sledge going home, Cass ignored Mrs Potts's monologue about what a lucky girl she was, and that she was not to even think about refusing to take up this opportunity, and if she did, she could go and live on the streets for all Mrs Potts cared. Cass could think of nothing but getting to the quay. *Let the tide be late tonight*, she prayed. As soon as they entered the City Gates, ignoring Mrs Potts's protests, Cass asked the sledge driver to stop. She jumped out and, without a word to her guardian, she slid her blades into her boots and tore along the streets.

The Quay of Thieves was thick with people. Cass weaved her way towards the Circus Boat's mooring, scanning the skyline for its distinctive bunting. She had nearly reached the mooring when, to her irritation, she got stuck behind a boy who really couldn't skate. He wobbled this way and that, blocking her path. Annoyed, Cass sped up to pass him, but then he swerved right in front of her, sending her crashing into him with a lurch. He caught her, preventing her from falling, and held her as if they were dancing together.

"Can't you watch where you are going?!" Cass cried furiously, but then froze when she saw the boy was Lord Enzo. And she had to admit that Tig was right. Up close he was without doubt the best-looking boy she had ever seen. He seemed to be made of brighter colours than the rest of the world with warm brown skin, a mop of vivid golden hair that was falling into his blue-green eyes, and a wide smile with very white teeth.

"Oh," he replied, smiling at the effect he was having on her. "I would have said it was you who should be looking where you were going. However, I apologise if it was my fault. I'm from the Islands so my skating is not so good." He gently let go of her arms.

At least he doesn't recognize me, Cass thought as she stammered, "I'm s-sorry too. It probably was my fault. But I must go, I'm late." She tore her eyes away from him to search for signs of the boat. *How Tig would have loved this*, she thought fleetingly.

"You're not looking for the Circus Boat, are you?" Enzo asked.

Cass nodded.

"I'm afraid it's just left," he replied. "About ten minutes ago."

Cass couldn't stop herself letting out a cry of frustration and anger, and her eyes filled with tears that refused to stay there and proceeded to slide down her cheeks. *I can't bear it*, she thought, feeling as if all her hopes had drained away like water down a plughole, leaving her nothing except the cold grey future of being companion to Madame Carpera.

She was so absorbed in her thoughts that she forgot about Enzo and was surprised when he said, "I'm sorry, did you have a friend on it? Someone you needed to say goodbye to?"

"No, I had an audition which I missed because … it's a long story," she replied, feeling acutely self-conscious of her tears and runny nose.

"And now the boat has gone for a whole year. How awful for you," he replied kindly, producing a beautiful silk handkerchief with a pattern of peacock feathers, and handed it to her. Cass took it gratefully and loudly blew her nose, making Enzo smile and Cass even more embarrassed. Just when she thought things couldn't get any worse, the boy she had thrown ice all over skated up to them.

"Hello again," he said to Cass with an amused smile. He was slight, with a shock of black hair and a severe, angular face. His high cheekbones and deep-set eyes might have intimidated Cass, were they not lightened with a kind smile.

"This is my cousin Rip," Enzo said. "I'm Enzo, and you are…"

"Cassandra," Cass replied sheepishly, wiping away her tears. "Sorry again for the other night," she said to Rip.

Rip laughed. "It's okay."

Enzo looked puzzled. "Do you two know each other?"

"Not really. We just had an encounter at the Circus," Rip replied.

Enzo burst out laughing. "Of course! I remember now. You're the girl who threw ice everywhere. Were you practising for a clowning audition? I can imagine that you're a complete natural."

Cass smiled weakly. She wasn't in the mood to be teased, even by a boy as handsome as Enzo. She just wanted to go home and cry without being watched.

"I must go," she said.

"Are you sure you wouldn't rather come aboard the Palace Ship and drink hot cacao?" Enzo asked.

"No thank you," Cass replied, suddenly desperate to leave. "I had better get back home." And with a hasty goodbye, she skated off. She was so distracted that she was halfway home before she realized she was still clutching the handkerchief, rolled up in a ball in her palm.

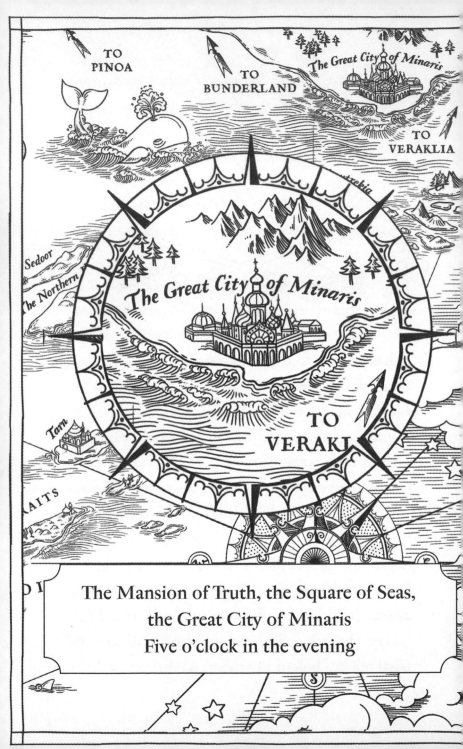

The Mansion of Truth, the Square of Seas,
the Great City of Minaris
Five o'clock in the evening

III

The Joyful Endeavour

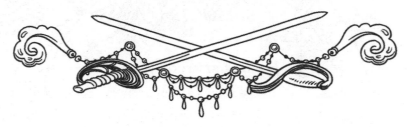

When she got to the Square of Seas, Cass decided she couldn't face going home, so she went to see Lin instead.

"Cass! What's the matter?" Lin asked, when she opened the door to her room and saw her friend's tear-stained face.

"I missed my audition. Mrs Potts made me late," Cass replied with a miserable sniff as Lin ushered her in. She plonked herself down in a chair by the fire as Lin's grey cat, Marvel, came and rubbed against her legs, then hopped on to her lap.

"Let me make you some tea while you tell me all about it," said Lin as she bustled around the room. "You still have that star over your head, you know, so something good must have happened, even if you don't recognize it now."

Cass snorted with disbelief and gave Lin an account of her terrible day.

"Oh, Cass, how devastating, and after all your hard work," she said sympathetically, handing her a china beaker of bitter tea.

"And now I am doomed to a life of lonely awfulness with Madame Carpera, stuck inside that gloomy house. Mrs Potts has told me I have to go."

"Perhaps it won't be so terrible?" Lin said diplomatically.

"It will be," Cass said matter-of-factly. "You know I cannot bear sitting still or being cooped up, and it will mean both."

"Come, let us think," said Lin. "There must be another option."

Cass sighed, thinking she might cry again.

"No, there isn't. The only thing I've ever been good at is acrobatics. And there's no other Circus in the Longest World apart from at Pingquing." Pingquing was the Great City of the Farthest Lands, and many months' journey from Minaris.

"No, you can't go there," Lin said decidedly.

Tears began to fall from Cass's eyes again. She pulled Enzo's handkerchief out of her pocket.

"That's very beautiful," Lin said, distracted by the sight of it.

"I know – it's …" She was about to tell Lin about Enzo but then found she wasn't in the mood to. "I borrowed it from someone."

Lin turned her attention back to Cass's future.

"If you can't do anything else, why don't you *go* somewhere else?" she suggested. "I know you've always wanted to see the world. Do you have any family anywhere?"

Cass shook her head. "My parents were both orphans, my father a Minarian one, and my mother from the Island of Women."

"Of course," Lin said, remembering. Then after a moment's thought she said, "Well, you could still go there, couldn't you?"

This hadn't occurred to Cass but Lin was right. After her mother died, Lady Sigh, who was the present head of the Island, had written to Mrs Potts, suggesting Cass make her home there. Mrs Potts had refused on her behalf.

"Do you know anything about the Island of Women?" Cass asked, thinking of the picture in her room. "Mrs Potts always says it's a very strange place."

"I don't think it's strange at all except, I suppose, for its lack of men. It's meant to be very beautiful and I love the fact that if you are a woman they will always let you stay there. However, I also know that magic is forbidden on the Island so it's not the place for me," Lin answered with a smile. "But it sounds perfect for you!" she joked. "I'm sure there would be plenty you could do – the orphanage must be huge and I know they grow a lot of crops. And you would probably have plenty of time to practise your acrobatics. You could come back to Minaris in a year when the Circus Boat returns. And you could use the money your parents left you for the passage. Surely Mrs Potts can't object to that."

"Mrs Potts will never let me go," Cass said sadly. "She is determined that I should work for Madame Carpera."

Lin sighed and said, "She does love you, you know. In her own way. And she is just doing what

40

she thinks is best."

Cass was in no mood to hear this. "She never listens to what I want," she replied. "It's all about her and being able to boast about me to her ghastly, gossipy friends like Mrs Cortini."

Lin glanced at the darkening sky out of the window. "I'm sorry, Cass, but I have to get ready for my clients. Why don't you try to delay Madame Carpera and then we can talk again tomorrow?"

Cass said goodbye and thanked her for the tea. She skated slowly across the square towards the Mansion of Fortune, thinking about Lin's idea of going to the Island of Women. It would solve all her problems and the thought of the picture in her room, the colours and the sunshine, drew her like a magnet.

She paused in the middle of the square by the statue of a famous magician and looked around. Much as she loved Tig and Lin, Cass knew she didn't belong there – how can an obtuse live surrounded by magic?

So on a whim she decided to skate back down to the port, just to see how much a voyage to the

Island of Women would cost.

Other ports in the Longest World had different systems but in Minaris, if a boat was offering passage, they put up a sign on the dock by the mooring. Cass walked along, scanning the wooden boards, which were scrawled with enticing-sounding destinations in the Near, Mid and Far Isles. The Island of Women lay in the south-western Mid Isles, so Cass was looking for a boat bound for Villuvia.

She came across one quickly, a smart little clipper with a smart captain to match, who wanted over five hundred silvers for passage. Cass knew that there was only a little over three hundred silvers of her parent's money left, sitting in the purse under the floorboards where Mrs Potts, who was not a believer in banks, kept it along with her own sizeable stash.

Cass was beginning to feel a creeping feeling of despair as she wandered along the Quay of Thieves, unable to find another boat headed that way, when she saw or rather heard the clamour of bleating goats, and found herself looking at a scruffy brig, optimistically named *The Joyful Endeavour*. It had a board in front of it saying, *Passages to Villuvia, via the Northern Passage – Loutrekia, Liversus, Ror, Sedoor, Parma, Consta, Villuvia.*

There was a cheerful-looking captain on board, smoking a baccy pipe and giving orders, who greeted her.

"Looking for passage, miss?"

"Yes," Cass replied. "I'm on my way to the Island of Women."

"Well, I can take you there easily enough. It'll take us about ten weeks and will cost you three hundred silvers for a shared cabin. But we leave this evening, in just over an hour, catching the last of the tide going out. Is that too soon for you?"

Cass hesitated. She had imagined herself leaving in a few days. But then, it would solve so many problems…

"No, that's perfect," she replied decisively.

The captain noticed Cass's citizen necklace around her neck. It only had a small fish charm dangling from it, which showed that although she was a True Minarian she was not yet of age. *Drat*, Cass thought, as she saw his eyes register it.

"You're not a runaway, are you?" he queried.

Cass's mind skipped over the letter she had forged for the Circus Boat. If she scrubbed out the bit about the Circus it would do, she decided.

"No, not at all – I can bring you a letter from my guardian. She's ill at the moment and keen for me to go to the Island of Women."

The captain inspected Cass again. She tried to look like she had an honest face.

"Very well. My name is Bemot by the way." And he put out his hand for Cass to shake.

"Cassandra. Cassandra Malvino," she replied and shook his.

"Nice to meet you, Cassandra. Well, you'd better hurry and fetch your things. Do you want me to send a boy with you?"

"No, I can manage, thank you," she replied.

"Very well. Remember, the tide waits for no one, so if you are not here I'm afraid I cannot wait for you."

Cass darted off, passing the Palace Ship. It looked like it was preparing to set sail too. She fleetingly thought of the handkerchief in her pocket. She should return it and apologize to Enzo for rushing off, but she had no time.

The Mansion of Fortune was remarkably silent for that time of day. Mrs Potts was drinking tea and Rimple's at her friend Mrs Cortini's, and Cass remembered that it was Tig's afternoon off. She knew she didn't have a moment to waste so she sprinted up the stairs to her room and fished out her duffel bag and the forged letter from under her bed.

After bidding the room a silent goodbye, she ran down to Mrs Potts's boudoir and retrieved the purse from under the floorboards. Then she sat and wrote her a short note of apology and explanation, which was perhaps the better for Cass not having thought about it too much. She folded and sealed it, and left it on the desk.

And then she took another piece of paper and wrote briefly to Tig, explaining what she was doing and promising to write further on the journey. She sped down to the kitchen with it and left it propped up on the mantelpiece before charging out of the basement door.

Lin was just between clients when Cass knocked lightly on her door.

"Hello again," she said.

Cass took a deep breath. "There's a boat that leaves for the Island of Women in less than half an hour," she said. "I've decided I should just go – otherwise Mrs Potts will never let me. I know it's sudden but I think it's for the best. So I've just come to say goodbye."

Lin was speechless for a moment.

"Oh, Cass, are you sure? This is a massive step to take. Why don't you wait and I'll talk to Mrs Potts with you, and we can plan this properly? You could write to Lady Sigh and…"

Cass shook her head and interrupted her, saying, "No, I need to go now. You said yourself that I had a star over my head – it is my destiny, I am sure of it. We both know I do not belong here amidst all this magic and I am certain that I do not belong with Madame Carpera either.

Honestly, it is for the best."

Lin didn't need to read her mind to see that she had decided. "I am going to miss you terribly, Cass," she said. "And I'd like you to take something of mine, so it will be easier for me to see you and what you're up to."

She pulled one of the many rings off her fingers. "Here, have this," she said, handing it to Cass. It was a simple plaited metal band. "I know it doesn't look much but I have worn it for so long that it has become a part of me, and I will miss you less if I know a part of me goes with you."

Cass was touched by Lin's kindness, and she hugged her tightly as she slipped the ring on to her finger. They said goodbye and then Cass rushed off, her boots clattering down the stairs.

Cass only just made it back to *The Joyful Endeavour* in time.

"I was about to give up on you," Captain Bemot said as he helped her aboard.

One of the sailors lifted the gangplank behind her while another started to crank up the anchor.

Cass leaned against the ship's rail and looked out over the harbour. The Palace Ship had gone. Perhaps she would see Enzo on the journey and she could return the handkerchief then. Otherwise she decided she would send it back to Tig, and she made herself smile imagining Tig's delight at receiving Lord Enzo's handkerchief.

As the boat sailed out of the harbour, the sun was setting behind Minaris, turning the sky the most glorious riot of pink, orange and violet streaks. The seventy-seven white towers, for which the city was famous, were silhouetted against the sky and the lamps in the Great Lighthouse shone out across the darkening water.

Cass felt a slight thud of misgiving in her stomach. The city was all she had ever known and she suddenly wondered whether she was crazy, leaving the familiar world behind her? But then she imagined herself sitting day after day in the twilight of Madame Carpera's sitting room and she knew she was making the right decision.

Maybe in a year's time, she told herself, she would

be sailing out of the harbour again, this time on the Circus Boat, and in the meantime the Island of Women would be an adventure, just not the one she had had in mind.

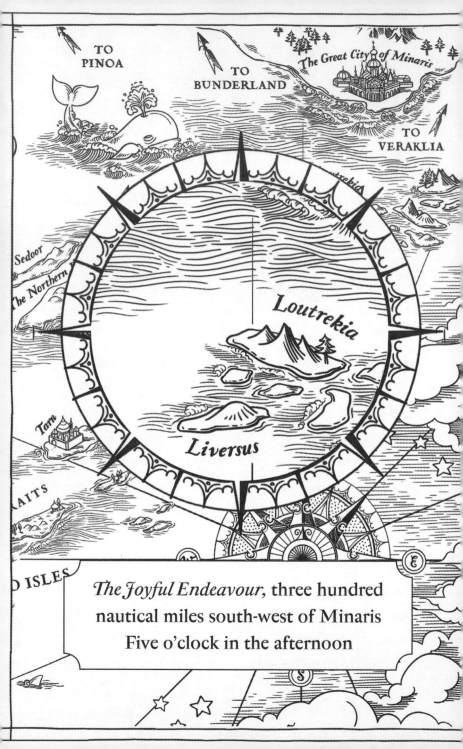

TO
PINOA

TO
BUNDERLAND

The Great City of Minaris

TO
VERAKLIA

Sedoor

The Northern

Loutrekia

Loutrekia

Tam

Liversus

AITS

ISLES

The Joyful Endeavour, three hundred
nautical miles south-west of Minaris
Five o'clock in the afternoon

IV

Caramel Nuts and Fighting Talk

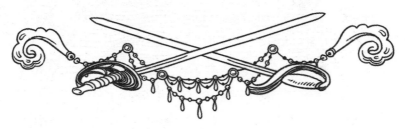

Despite having grown up in one of the greatest ports in the Longest World, Cass had barely been on a boat and had certainly never been out of sight of land. She had wondered before whether the boat's constant movement would make her sick or whether she would find being out in the vast grey sea frightening, but as it turned out she had a strong stomach and she found the empty, changeable sea exhilarating. She felt a keen sense of excitement and possibility at her adventure that even *The Joyful Endeavour's* tatty, peeling paint, and constant bleating of the goats couldn't dampen.

The first few days of the voyage were so bitterly

cold that Cass and the other passengers stayed huddled around the stove in the cheerful little main cabin, reading, writing letters or playing cards. Cass's conscience was still pricking her about Mrs Potts, knowing that the old lady would be angry but also hurt by her running away, and she spent several hours composing another apologetic and explanatory letter. Cass's fellow travellers were a mix of traders and Minarians visiting relatives, who spent most of their time complaining about the weather and fretting about pirates, who apparently were an increasing threat in the Mid Isles. They paid Cass little attention and she them. The only person she really spoke to apart from the crew was Elsba, the lady with whom she was sharing a cabin.

There was a quiet stillness about Elsba that Cass found calming and comforting. She was quite the opposite, Cass decided, of Mrs Potts and her incessant chatter. And it wasn't just the way Elsba looked, which was soothingly unremarkable; she could have been any age between thirty and fifty and her mocha skin, brown eyes and black hair all had a blue-greyness to them that made her fade into the background. Her clothes were the dullest

Cass had ever seen and she held herself with a shy stoop. Her voice was soft, her laugh gentle and yet there was a strength about her that was slightly at odds with her appearance. This intrigued Cass but Elsba only asked a few questions about her acrobatics and Dr Bromver's exercises that Cass was still doing religiously in their tiny cabin, so Cass did not feel she could quiz her in return. They talked mostly of the boat and the weather and other impersonal matters, and when Cass thought of her later on, she realized she knew almost nothing about Elsba, other than she was a midwife and was travelling to Villuvia, the large island near the Island of Women that she called home. Cass asked Elsba about the Island of Women, but she had little to add to what Cass already knew – it was very beautiful, with a slightly mysterious community of women who did a lot of charitable works and she was sure that Cass would be very happy there.

The *Joyful Endeavour*'s first stop a week or so later was at the small port on the Island of Loutrekia in the Near Isles. It was late afternoon and Cass was teaching Elsba the Minarian game of Happiness when she saw lights through the porthole. With a shriek of excitement she ran over to the window.

"It's land!" she cried.

"It is indeed," Elsba replied. "It's Loutrekia. We stop here until the tide tomorrow afternoon, so shall we go and explore?"

"Yes please!" Cass cried, totally over-excited. "Let's go on deck!"

They both bundled themselves up in their furs and went out into the fading light as the boat lumbered between the harbour walls into the busy little port. They watched the buildings coming into view with their twinkling lights reflecting prettily in the water. The harbour was crowded with boats, big and small, but there was one so huge that it towered over the others like an elephant in the middle of a herd of cows. It was the Palace Ship.

"Oh look, Lord Bastien is here," Elsba remarked, confirming the ship's reality. "There is sure to be a party tonight," she added with her gentle smile.

Cass laughed. Lord Bastien was known mockingly as the Party Protector and the Minarian news sheets were always attacking him for neglecting the Islands and for his extravagance. There were persistent rumours that he was bankrupt, and there was often talk of King Lycus replacing him, despite the fact that the post had always been passed from father to son. But politics were not foremost in Cass's mind at that moment. Rather, she was thinking that she should return Enzo's handkerchief to him, and how much fun it would be to go aboard the Palace Ship.

"I must just get something from the cabin," she mumbled to Elsba and dived back down the rickety stairs as the boat manoeuvred towards a gap between moored vessels, the goats bleating fiercely.

Cass retrieved the handkerchief from her trunk. It was rather creased but she decided it would do, hurriedly smoothing it out and shoving it in her pocket. She also remembered the letters that she had written to Mrs Potts and Tig, and scooped those up too.

Once the boat was anchored and tied up, Cass and Elsba jumped out on to the slippery white marble cobbles. It was still freezing but there was no ice or snow, and as they walked around the harbour, Cass noticed just a tang of spring in the air mixing with the smell of wood smoke and oil lamps.

Loutrekia was fortunately situated at the convergence of several shipping routes and had long been a wealthy trading post. It was always busy and that evening was no exception. Cass and Elsba linked arms to avoid getting separated in the jostling crowds. They were so used to being on the boat that the land was still swaying beneath them. There was some of Minaris's grandeur in its elaborately painted house facades, Cass thought, but then as soon as you heard the beat of the island Bara music spilling out from the inns you were in no doubt that Minaris was miles away.

"My stomach will not wait another moment for supper," Elsba announced, leading them over to an inn. Rather than trying to find a space inside, they paid a silver each for a soft floury yellow pancake stuffed with juicy slices of meat and fried onions. They ate huddled by a brazier with a clear view of the Palace Ship. The party on board looked like it had already started, judging by the stream of people parading up the gangplank.

"Come, let us walk," Elsba announced. "It's much too cold not to. And I am desperate for some of those caramel nuts I can smell. I think the stall is over there."

Elsba bought a scoop and they dawdled along, looking at the stalls that were selling goods from all over the Islands. Elsba made some more small purchases – a bar of milk soap, a jar of honeycomb and a small bunch of melliflet flowers, which she explained with a laugh would drive the smell of goat from their cabin. As they walked they were slowly but surely drawing nearer and nearer to the great bulk of the Palace Ship. And despite the noise of the crowds around them, Cass could hear the tantalizing sound of music and laughter drifting down from it.

As they approached, she told Elsba her story about the handkerchief, finishing with, "… so you see, I really do think I should try and return it." She produced the handkerchief from her pocket.

Elsba touched the silk softly between her fingers. "It's beautiful," she said. "If it were mine I'd want it back, even if I were a lord. Shall I wait for you?"

"Oh no," Cass replied quickly. She didn't want to have to return to Elsba if Enzo asked her to stay for the party.

Elsba nodded, a half-smile on her face.

"You go on then," she said. "I need to buy a few more things. I'll meet you back at the boat."

A broad gangplank led down from the ship to a quay and at the bottom of it stood the girl who had been with Enzo, Bastien and Rip in the Circus tent. She was in her late teens and beautifully dressed in a white fur coat. She had blue-black hair, fair skin and bright blue eyes and reminded Cass of an expensive china doll Mrs Potts had bought her when she was little. Cass had never much liked it; it was too precious to play with and what was the point of a toy that you could only look at? The girl stared questioningly at Cass as she walked towards her, and Cass felt acutely aware of her scruffy furs and battered old boots.

"Can I help you?" the girl asked Cass imperiously.

Oddly, her rudeness made Cass bolder.

"I have something to return to Lord Enzo," she replied just as snootily.

The girl narrowed her eyes. "You can give it to me. I will make sure he gets it." Some people arrived behind Cass. "Now, can you move out of the way please?"

Cass felt her opportunity slipping away. The

other people, rich merchants and their wives, were ushered up the gangplank with broad smiles and greetings. Cass felt very out of place, she had been stupid to come, stupid to think…

"Well?" said the girl, sensing she had won. "Where is this thing to be returned to Lord Enzo?"

Cass produced the handkerchief.

"A handkerchief?" The girl laughed. "He's a lord! I think he can afford to lose a few handkerchiefs. Why don't you keep it as a souvenir of your time together?" she added nastily.

Cass felt herself go bright red. She had never hated anyone as much as she hated this girl at that moment and she would not be beaten by her.

"I have plenty of my own handkerchiefs, thank you. I'd like to return it to him, and in person too so that I can be sure that he gets it," she replied tartly. "If Lord Enzo is busy with the party then I can come back in the morning."

"Yes, why don't you?" the girl replied. "But in the meantime please could you move out of the way – our guests are arriving."

Cass walked away with her head held high and a swagger in her step to hide any suggestion of defeat. But she couldn't face going straight back to the boat, so she wandered around the harbour and spent a silver on a coral bracelet and a hot buttered bun. But as the night drew in, the crowds became more unruly, alarming Cass, and she started to make her way back to *The Joyful Endeavour*. She was nearly there when she saw a sign for a Postage Office and remembered the letters in her pocket. It would only take a few minutes to send them, she thought, and then they would go on the mail boat first thing in the morning.

The office was up a narrow alley, but Cass had only walked a few steps along it when a hand shot out from nowhere, grabbing her. Before she could cry out, another hand, sweaty and dirty-smelling, clamped itself over her mouth in a swift, practised manoeuvre and she found herself being dragged into a small unlit courtyard. Another figure appeared in front of her. A woman, Cass could just about make out in the gloom, who began to search through Cass's pockets for her purse.

A jolt of fury passed through her. She was not going to let them take what remained of her parents' money. So she started to try to kick the woman and stamp on the feet of the figure who held her.

"Keep still!" a man's voice instructed – the man who held her. But Cass had no intention of making it easy for them and started to buck and squirm with all her might. She succeeded in making the man loosen his grip just enough for Cass to open her mouth slightly and bite down on his hand hard.

"AAGHH!" he cried, moving it for a second, although his other arm still held her tight.

"HELP! HELP!" Cass managed to cry before the hand was back over her mouth. And then she felt the woman's hand close over her purse.

"Got it!" she shouted to the man, who, in another practised move, swept Cass's legs out from under her, so she crashed to the ground as they both darted towards the entrance of the courtyard.

But they were cut off by a third figure appearing, blocking their escape, who launched itself at the woman, ripping the purse off her and sending her flying across the courtyard. The man gave a shout of fury and flung himself at the figure. But to Cass's amazement, the figure, without appearing to move, got the better of the man, and he too was sprawling on the floor a moment later.

"Come," the figure said in a calm voice to Cass.

Cass didn't need to be told twice, and jumped up off the floor and followed the figure back into the alley.

"Th-thank you so much," she stuttered.

"It's nothing," the figure replied, turning around and pressing the purse back into Cass's hand. To Cass's amazement she recognized who it was. It was Elsba.

Cass was so exhausted by her ordeal that she slept late the following morning. Elsba woke her with a cup of bitter tea and a jam tart from breakfast.

"How are you?" she asked kindly.

Cass was a bit stiff but otherwise fine. She was far more interested in another matter.

"How did you learn to fight like that?"

"Older brothers," Elsba replied with a laugh. And then when she could see that such an answer was not going to satisfy Cass, she went on. "I actually learned on the Island of Women."

"Really?" Cass said, intrigued.

Elsba nodded. "Yes, quite a few girls from Villuvia go over for lessons in science and mathematics and those sort of things, but also sometimes for –" she hesitated slightly before saying vaguely – "other things."

"Will I be able to learn to fight there?" Cass asked excitedly.

"I don't see why not," Elsba replied. "The teacher is a woman named Pela. All the girls are taught how to defend themselves – Lady Sigh thinks it is very important – and then some are taught more – sword fighting and other forms of combat." She paused, considering Cass for a moment. "You might be very good at it, with your acrobatics. By the way, did you get to see Bastien's son last night?"

"No, I said I would go back today," said Cass.

Elsa looked puzzled. "The Palace Ship has already gone – it sailed soon after dawn."

Cass felt a jab of fury about being lied to by the black-haired girl.

"There is every chance they will be in Liversus," Elsba said optimistically, noticing how Cass had taken the news. "We'll be there in three days' time."

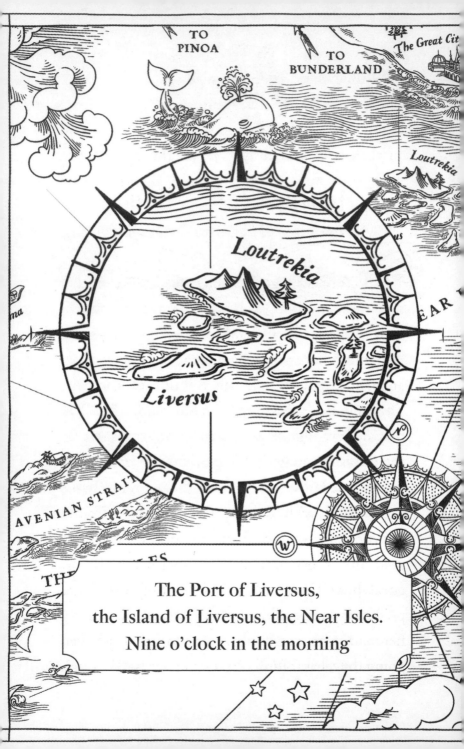

The Port of Liversus,
the Island of Liversus, the Near Isles.
Nine o'clock in the morning

V

An Invitation to Dine

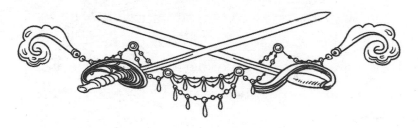

"There are hot springs here, just up the mountain, apparently," Elsba told Cass over breakfast. *The Joyful Endeavour* had sailed into Liversus late on the previous evening. "I thought I might go to bathe in them this morning. Would you like to come?"

Cass used to visit the Bath House in Minaris every week with Mrs Potts. It was a splendid building; a labyrinth of steamy rooms, lined with gold and green tiles, that smelled deliciously of eucalyptus. Cass used to love standing under the pounding water of the showering room, washing her hair with mud soap, knowing that she was going to feel absolutely clean afterwards. Although she had washed as best she could on the boat, she suddenly felt filthy.

"Yes please," she replied.

The hot springs were a short donkey ride up a steep, stony path up which weaved between the houses that spilled down from the mountain behind. As Elsba seemed absorbed in her own thoughts, Cass focused instead on the view of the green hills ahead of her, which were cloaked in spring flowers and bisected by narrow, rushing streams.

The Bath House proved to be a small wooden building and to the side of it, out in the open, Cass could just glimpse the steaming, milky-blue waters of a rocky pool. The lady in charge tied up the donkeys and beckoned Cass and Elsba inside, showing them where to change their clothes and giving them each a couple of large linen bathing sheets and a bar of grainy green soap.

Hot springs bubbled their way to the surface all over the Near and Mid Isles, but Cass had never seen them before and was enchanted by the tree-fringed pool. They both changed discreetly and then, using the linen sheets for modesty, lowered themselves into the pool. Cass wasn't deliberately looking at Elsba but she happened to glance over just as she was dropping her sheet. Cass was amazed to see a tattoo of a figure of eight etched on Elsba's back, right between her shoulder blades. Cass had only ever seen tattoos before on sailors and traders from the Far Isles, who gathered to drink and fight in the rougher inns in Minaris. Elsba seemed as far from them as a person could possibly be.

The donkeys took a different path down and the port of Liversus was spread out beneath them like a fan. Over on the far side of the harbour, some distance away from *The Joyful Endeavour*, Cass spied a large ship. It had such a distinctive shape that even from high above, Cass could clearly see it was the Palace Ship.

"Oh, not you again," the dark-haired girl drawled at Cass. She was standing on the side of the quay by the Palace Ship with Rip.

"Hello, Cassandra," Rip greeted her with a

grin. "I don't think that you have been formally introduced to my charming friend Ornella? Ornella, Cassandra, Cassandra, Ornella. There, now you can be the best of friends."

"I am so delighted to meet you," Cass replied with exaggerated politeness and a curtsy as if they were at a ball together. She was pleased to see how annoyed Ornella looked.

But Ornella took her revenge.

"Have you followed us all the way here to bring back Enzo's handkerchief? Have you been sleeping with it under your pillow?" she asked spitefully.

Cass flushed slightly, replying, "No, I just happen to be travelling the same way, on a merchant's boat," she said, waving in the general direction of *The Joyful Endeavour*.

A glint of amusement flicked in the girl's eyes. "You're not by any chance travelling on the goat boat, are you?"

Cass felt herself blush even more and Ornella let out peals of laughter.

"How incredibly glamorous!" she mocked.

"Ornella!" Rip said. "Why don't you come with

me, Cassandra?" he went on. "Enzo's just here, on the ship."

Cass couldn't resist a broad smirk at Ornella as she followed Rip up the gangplank.

Enzo was standing on deck with a woman of about thirty years old. She had long red hair hanging in a heavy plait down her back and a fair, freckly face. She was dressed like a man in breeches, a shirt and waistcoat.

Cass was worried that Enzo wouldn't remember who she was but her fears were unfounded.

"It's my clumsy friend," he said, grinning at Cass and flicking his hair out of his eyes. "What are you doing here?"

Cass suddenly felt shy and she found herself stammering,

"I s-saw your boat and I j-just wanted to return your handkerchief." She pulled it out of her pocket and handed it to him.

"You've come all the way from Minaris to do that?" Enzo asked, taking it from her, his face a mixture of amusement and amazement.

"No, no." Cass smiled awkwardly, feeling foolish. "I'm travelling to the Island of Women and this is one of the stops on the way."

"Why are you going to the Island of Women?" asked Rip.

"Um, it's a long story," Cass replied, grateful to look at someone less dazzling than Enzo. "As you know, I missed my Circus audition and so my terrible fate was to work as a companion to an old lady. I couldn't bear the thought of being cooped up like that, so instead I decided to spend a year on the Island of Women, before I can audition again."

"Did you run away?" Enzo asked, looking impressed.

"Sort of," Cass admitted with a shrug.

The woman in the breeches came forward. "I'm sorry to eavesdrop but running away to the Island of Women sounds very adventurous!" she said. "Let me introduce myself, my name is Idaliz."

Cass shook her hand.

"It's nice to meet you, Cass," Idaliz said. "In between doing other things, I teach these two sword fighting."

Cass thought with a smile about Madame Carpera and Mrs Potts's view on female sword fighters and replied, "Really? That sounds like fun."

"Well, it is sometimes, depending on how hard these boys are concentrating. Tell me, what were you auditioning to be at the Circus?"

"An acrobat," Cass replied.

"You are joking!" Enzo teased her.

"Oh, then you must show us your audition piece," Idaliz exclaimed.

"Yes, this I have to see," Enzo said.

Cass was never one to resist a challenge and as she had pantaloons on under her dress, she threw herself into a quick-fire display of tumbling and cartwheels, earning a round of loud applause and cheers from her audience.

"That was very impressive," Idaliz said. "I was just about to give these boys a lesson focusing on balance. As yours is so amazing, will you stay and help me?"

"I would love that," Cass replied, thinking about Elsba and her fighting.

"Excellent," said Idaliz and threw Cass a wooden sword, which she caught neatly. "Let us begin by standing on one leg and doing a few simple moves with the sword."

It quickly became apparent that although Rip and Enzo were both reasonably good at sword fighting, Cass was much better than either of them, despite having only picked up a sword for the first time that afternoon. This seemed to amuse Rip, but Enzo was clearly annoyed by it, to such a degree that Cass curbed her natural desire to show off so as not to irritate him too much. Idaliz had no such qualms about winding Enzo up and lavishly praised Cass.

When they had finished, Idaliz shook her hand, saying, "Now, please excuse me, I have to go and pack. I have business in Pinoa so I leave tonight on a boat to Huertn on the mainland. But I hope I will see you again one day. Goodbye, Cass." And with a quick bow, she was gone.

Later that afternoon, back on board *The Joyful Endeavour*, Cass received a note, delivered by a liveried messenger from the Palace Ship. Intrigued, she tore it open.

Lord Bastien invites you to dine with him and other friends tonight onboard the Palace Ship at the seventh hour of the evening.

Cass was so amazed that it took a moment for her face to split into a huge grin. After the fun of the lesson, she had reluctantly left the Palace Ship thinking that as *The Joyful Endeavour* and the Palace Ship were on different courses, she was unlikely to see Enzo or Rip again. How wrong she had been!

"Do you have anything to wear?" Elsba asked Cass, when she showed her the note.

Cass thought. There was her blue silk dress that she had worn to Madame Carpera's. She pulled it out for Elsba to inspect.

"I think that's perfect," Elsba said. "Shall I help you with your hair?"

Cass quickly glanced in the mirror. She hadn't combed it since they left Minaris and washing it at the springs had turned it into even more of a bird's nest than normal.

"Yes please," she said, fishing a brush, comb and bottle of Magical Untangle Pomade out of the bottom of her bag.

It took Elsba the best part of an hour to comb all the knots out of Cass's hair. They both kept apologizing to the other – Cass for the fact that she could hardly sit still she was so excited, and for the terrible state of her hair, and Elsba for pulling it. At last the final knot was untangled and Elsba brushed it for Cass until it shone like gold.

"You have such beautiful hair,'" Elsba remarked. "Shall I put it up for you? Or shall I just pull these bits back? I could plait them."

Cass nodded and Elsba got to work. She fetched the tiny bunch of melliflet flowers that were in a glass by her bed and wove them into Cass's hair. When she was finished, she held up the glass. Cass couldn't help but smile at her reflection, she looked so much better.

"Thank you, Elsba," she said.

The bell rang for supper, which meant Cass was late. She pulled her tatty furs around her.

"Enjoy yourself!" Elsba gave her a kiss on her cheek. "I won't wait up."

"Thank you and thank you so much for my hair," Cass said, as she ran out of their cabin.

Ornella was standing, as usual, at the bottom of the gangplank, greeting people. She waved Cass up without acknowledging her. As soon as Cass's foot touched the deck, servants swooped down on her from all sides,

"This way, miss, please. The party is in the Gold Room tonight."

"May I take your furs, miss?"

"May I offer you some summer wine?"

Cass found herself in a large low-ceilinged room, lit by scores of candles. Two huge stoves burned at either end, making it very warm, and the air was thick with cigarillo smoke. Cass, who thought of parties only in terms of Mrs Potts's genteel gatherings, or the formal Minarian merchants' balls that she and Tig used to spy on, was amazed by the sight before her. The floor was lined with thick rugs and people sat in groups on piles of cushions and low sofas, chattering noisily, shrieking with laughter. The women were all dressed in bright silks, many in breeches or pantaloons, and almost as many were smoking. Mrs Potts would have been horrified, Cass thought, and she looked down at her demure, sleeved silk dress, feeling exquisitely frumpy and rather hot. She took a sip of her icy summer wine gratefully and craned her neck, looking for Enzo or Rip. Enzo was on the opposite side of the room and when he saw her, he came over.

"I don't believe it, you've brushed your hair," he teased.

Cass felt shy again of Enzo and tried to think of a clever response. But her mind was blank.

"Er, yes," she muttered, thinking how incredibly dull she sounded.

"You look lovely," Enzo reassured her. "And was Ornella polite to you?"

"She was."

"Good. Now you must follow me," he said.

"Why?" Cass queried.

"Because my father wants to meet you," Enzo replied.

Cass felt a twinge of nerves as they approached the Lord Protector of the Islands. He was lying on a sofa, smoking a hookah, surrounded by a crowd of people. They parted to make way for Enzo and Cass. Enzo introduced her and as she bowed politely to Lord Bastien, she could feel everyone looking at her curiously.

"Ah yes," Bastien said in his rich, deep voice. "Please come and sit with me before supper." Space was made for Cass to perch on an emerald-green silk stool next to the sofa, as Bastien continued.

"Enzo has told me all about you," he said, waving the end of his hookah expansively. "You are on your way to the Island of Women and you are a very talented acrobat."

"Yes, thank you, sire," Cass replied politely.

"And what's all this I hear about you missing your audition for the Circus Boat?"

"Yes, I hope I will be luckier next year," she replied as cheerfully as she could.

"But a year is such a long time at your age, isn't it?" Bastien said sympathetically and Cass nodded. "Is it your greatest dream?" he asked, looking at her intently.

"It is," she replied, blushing slightly.

"In that case I have an idea. You may not know this but the Circus Boat will be in Tarn at the same time as us. Ravellous owes me a favour so I can speak to him for you – I am sure I can persuade him to give you an audition. Dreams are so important, my dear."

"That is very kind of you, sire, but I am on a boat that sails down the Northern Passage, so I will not be going to Tarn," Cass replied, unable to keep the disappointment out of her voice.

Bastien tutted. "That is such a shame," he replied.

A gong announced supper and a procession of servants appeared with trays of food.

"I am afraid I must go and speak to some of my other guests now, my dear, but we will talk again later. And in the meantime, Enzo will look after you." Then Bastien, in a surprisingly quick movement, got up from the sofa and began his progression around the room.

Enzo spoke to Cass for a couple of minutes before saying he would fetch her another drink. But instead of returning, Enzo made his way to the other side of the room. Soon he was lolling on a cushion next to a pretty girl wearing an elegant dress of purple silk.

I obviously bored him, Cass thought, flushing

with humiliation. She heard someone say that the girl was the daughter of the richest merchant in Liversus and they had just been robbed. *She doesn't look too upset about it*, Cass thought meanly, watching her giggle and simper at Enzo.

Bastien's talk of the Circus Boat had brought back her feelings of disappointment and to her embarrassment, she felt herself having to fight back tears. She was relieved when a servant stooped down with a tray and Cass took a bowl of the food offered to her and another glass of summer wine. She tried to look as if she were perfectly happy on her own and fully occupied with the business of eating her supper. Ornella walked past.

"Enjoying the party?" she asked spitefully.

"Yes thank you," Cass replied tartly and continued to eat her food, gazing determinedly into her bowl.

"Hello," a voice said close to her and Cass looked up to see Rip.

"Can I sit with you?" he asked, and when Cass readily agreed, he sat down on the sofa vacated by his uncle.

Cass felt embarrassed at being deserted by Enzo,

which made her shy with Rip. But he asked her such gentle questions about home and why she wanted to become an acrobat that she relaxed. He was even easier to talk to than Tig, she decided.

"So what was it like growing up surrounded by magic?" he asked.

"Well, slightly strange once it became clear that I was an obtuse," Cass replied.

"Are you really?" Rip asked. "That's very unusual."

"Yes, and very embarrassing when you are the daughter of a famous fortune teller," she said.

Rip laughed. "I'm told it's a gift in itself."

As trays of sticky sweets and ices were being brought round, Enzo returned.

"Has Rip been telling you about the Island of Women?" he asked, plonking himself down next to them.

Cass looked surprised.

"I was born there," Rip explained.

Cass decided that they were teasing her and gave them a sceptical look.

"Really," Rip assured her. "I lived there with my mother. Look at my citizen necklace." And he pulled it out from under his shirt, showing Cass that there were indeed two charms on it – one showing Bastien's crest, which gave Rip citizenship to all the Islands, and a butterfly.

"It's the Venderven butterfly, which is only found on the Island," he explained.

"But you're a boy!" Cass protested.

"Boys are allowed to live there until they are nine," Rip explained. "My mother died when I was seven and then I stayed on for a while, before Bastien came for me. And I have been on the Palace Ship ever since, working as the navigator."

"He has the sharpest eyes in the Longest World," Enzo said. "Don't you think he looks a little like a hawk?"

Before Cass could reply, a deep voice above them said, "There you all are." And they scrambled to their feet as Bastien appeared.

"Now, my dear, I've been thinking," he said to Cass. "There is nothing an old man like me enjoys so much as the company of young people, and as you are getting on so famously with my boys an idea has come to me. I have been looking for someone to help Ornella with a backlog of paperwork. Poor Ornella acts as my social secretary and she is completely overwhelmed." He paused. "So I wondered whether you might be persuaded to sail with us instead of on your current boat. I would pay you, of course, as well as giving you passage. And that way, I can speak to Ravellous for you in Tarn. If by any chance Ravellous won't take you, then we are sailing down the Avenian Straits towards Villuvia and will be passing right by the Island of Women."

Cass felt dizzy with astonishment. She noticed Rip and Enzo exchange a questioning glance.

"You don't have to decide now, my dear," Bastien said. "Think about it overnight. We will sail for Bunt at midday tomorrow. Rip, please show Cass the cabin she would share with Ornella."

Cass followed Rip, still feeling amazed by Bastien's offer. She had only ever heard of his selfishness before but here Bastien was showing her great kindness. It didn't quite add up.

She was, however, entirely distracted by the sight of the cabin. Cass had never seen such a luxurious bedroom before. Like the rest of the ship, its walls and ceilings were covered in shiny wood panelling, which smelled soothingly of beeswax. Thick carpet covered the floor and there was a stove, a proper window and a wardrobe. Slung across half of it was a white silk hammock piled high with pale pink silk eiderdowns and pillows. There was, Cass decided, easily room for another one. Even the thought of being stuck with Ornella day and night didn't put Cass off in the slightest and she sighed with delight.

The party was finishing and a servant appeared with Cass's furs. Enzo had disappeared so she just said goodbye to Rip. *I must thank Bastien,* she thought. He was surrounded by guests saying goodbye. Cass went over, hovering uncertainly, but then he saw her. Reaching between the other guests, he took her hand, saying, "I do so hope you will consider my offer seriously, my dear. You would be such a welcome addition to our merry band of wanderers."

"Thank you, sire," Cass replied, her mind already made up.

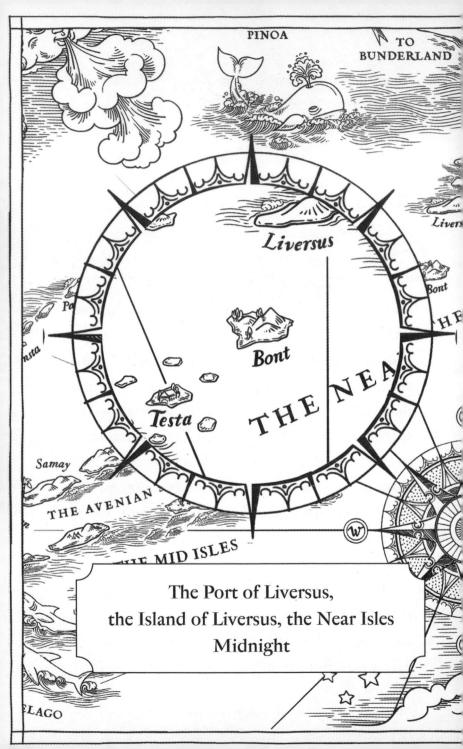

PINOA

TO
BUNDERLAND

Liversus

Livers

Bont

Pa

Bont

sta

THE NEA

Testa

Samay

THE AVENIAN

THE MID ISLES

W

The Port of Liversus,
the Island of Liversus, the Near Isles
Midnight

LAGO

VI

The View from the Crow's Nest

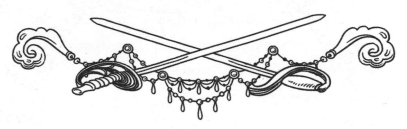

Elsba stirred and mumbled a sleepy "hello" when Cass, in a state of euphoria, tiptoed back into their cabin. On the walk home, everything had fallen into place for her. The Palace Ship was clearly her destiny, and the star over her head the night before she left Minaris was because she had met Enzo and Bastien at the Circus. Cass was so bursting with her news, she couldn't stop herself blurting it all out.

"The most astonishing thing has happened. The Palace Ship is sailing near the Island of Women and the Lord Protector has offered me passage with them. But best of all, when we dock in Tarn, the Circus Boat will be there too and he will ask Ravellous to audition me."

Elsba rubbed her eyes as she sat up in her hammock, looking suitably surprised.

"It's so generous and nice of him," Cass went on happily.

"Really?" Elsba questioned. "Lord Bastien is not known for his kindness – he mostly does things that profit himself," she said, echoing Cass's former thoughts.

"I agree that I have heard that about him too. But it only goes to show that you cannot judge people by their reputations. Also he does want me to help Ornella, his social secretary, with some paperwork," she explained.

Not wishing to pour cold water on Cass's pleasure, Elsba asked, "When does the Palace Ship sail?"

"In the morning," Cass said, getting into her hammock.

"So soon! Well, we'd both better get some sleep then – good night," Elsba said, turning over.

Cass felt as if her brain was on fire with excitement and that she would be awake all night.

But the gentle rocking of the hammock sent her into a strange half-sleep, where she had vivid dreams of Tig and Mrs Potts. When she woke with a start, she could see the sun was just coming up through the porthole. She crept quietly out of her hammock. Half an hour later she was washed, dressed and packed, and trying to concentrate on reading a book. When Elsba woke, she dressed and helped Cass up the stairs with her duffel bag. They ate their last breakfast together and Cass then explained her change of plan to Captain Bemot, who looked as surprised as everyone else.

"Which way are they sailing?" he asked.

"Their next stop is Bunt."

The captain nodded. "They will be going down the Avenian Straits, which is a different route from us, so you won't be able to change your mind."

Cass suppressed a smile. Much as she liked Captain Bemot, why would she ever choose to travel on his goat boat rather than on the Palace Ship?

"I will help Cass carry her luggage over there," Elsa said diplomatically.

"We sail in half an hour so if you want to go

running off with the Lord Protector too, please come and tell me," the captain joked to Elsba.

"Oh look," Cass cried. "There's no need to help me." And she was right. Two men, dressed in Bastien's livery, walked on to the boat. So sure had the Lord Protector been of Cass's response that he had sent them.

"Are you ready, miss? Is this all your luggage?" they asked and when Cass nodded they picked up her bag and walked off with it towards the Palace Ship.

Bubbling with excitement, she flung her arms round Elsba. "Goodbye."

"Goodbye and good luck," Elsba said, giving her a hug with a worried smile.

And so Cass went to the Palace Ship, practically skipping with delight.

Her stay didn't start particularly well. She had barely opened her bag when Ornella appeared in the doorway to their cabin.

"Don't start unpacking yet. I want to check that

you can read and write first," she said snidely.

Cass ignored the insult. She was wary of being rude to Ornella in case she ran complaining to Bastien, so she replied politely, "Of course."

Ornella looked surprised at Cass's lack of comeback.

"Come with me," she ordered, leading Cass to a tiny, overflowing office. It had space for little more than a desk and a couple of chairs. "I have a huge pile of urgent correspondence to deal with as well as fifty invitations to write for our next stop. I want you to write the invitations but your handwriting needs to be perfect. Pull up a chair." Ornella made room for Cass to sit next to her at the desk and showed her how to write an invitation, then watched as she copied it.

Cass did it carefully, in her best calligraphic hand that she had learned at Mrs Papworth's Academy. She could see Ornella was impressed, although she just gave Cass a curt nod of approval. "Here is the list of guests. Write them all and then I will check and seal them."

They sat together all morning, Ornella sighing over a stack of unpaid bills, while Cass worked her way through the invitations. Although the older girl was still abrupt and eye-wateringly rude to Cass, her frostiness thawed fractionally.

From Liversus, the Palace Ship passed into the Mid Isles and made its meandering way towards the Avenian Straits, stopping at every major island on the way and some of the minor ones too. For it was Bastien's duty as Lord Protector to tour around the Islands and meet with the mayors and other local worthies, and listen to their concerns. These meetings were meant to be calm, business-like affairs, and Cass knew that Bastien's father, who had been an honourable and diligent Protector, had sailed quietly around, only giving the occasional modest reception.

Bastien however was not his father, and instead he threw an endless succession of riotous parties that he filled with the most amusing people he could find to dilute, as he said to Cass "the worthy whingers". But he didn't entirely succeed and Cass still overheard, as she was helping Ornella at the parties, a good deal of disgruntled muttering about Bastien and his tolerance of the slavers and his lack of action over the pirates. The latter's attacks on the merchants' ships and wealthier island ports were beginning to have serious consequences, Cass gathered. Trade was the lifeblood of the Islands and without it, the economy would grind to a halt. Thank goodness, they all whispered in undertones, that King Lycus had dispatched some naval ships to try and catch them.

Only a little over a month had passed since Cass left Minaris, but she couldn't believe how her circumstances had changed, even if life on board the Palace Ship was not quite the one long sword-fighting lesson she had hoped. In fact, Cass decided, it was probably rather like being on the Circus Boat. The parties were like performances but between them, when they were at sea, everyone worked extremely hard.

Rip, as the ship's navigator, spent his time either with the captain or in the crow's nest, or mucking in with the sailors. But he was very kind to Cass, seeking her out if he had a spare moment and chiding Ornella if she was being too rude to her, and Cass found herself looking for excuses to go and chat to him. Bastien also made a point of speaking to Cass whenever he saw her, asking her warmly how she was getting on. And Enzo was friendly enough too, in a distant way.

After Cass had been on board for a couple of weeks, they stopped at the small Island of Testa. Testa was known as the Star of the Mid Isles, partly because of its pale rocky cliffs and white stony beaches but also because it was set in the middle of a constellation-like arrangement of other small islands. The ship docked in the main port, which lay on its west side. Cass knew from Ornella that the plan was to stay there for a night and, as usual, throw a large party to announce Bastien's presence.

Each day the weather grew a little warmer, until the moment, as they pulled into the port and were sheltered from the wind, that Cass was actually hot. She peered out through the office porthole, and could see a different Mid Isles world had appeared. The sea was calm and clear and a delightful patchwork of pale greens and blues. The houses were a tumbledown mix of white stone, with a riot of pink and orange flowers cascading over them. Behind were not the forbidding grey mountains of the Near Isles, but gentle green hills. How amazing it was, Cass thought for the umpteenth time, to see so much of the Longest World.

Later, as the light was beginning to fade and the party was well under way, Cass weaved her way across the crowded deck to bring a rich noble and his wife to Bastien. When she reached him, she was about to turn and go back to help Ornella, but Enzo caught her arm.

"Find Rip, will you?" he whispered to Cass. "My father is getting annoyed that he is not here. He is probably in the crow's nest. Are you okay to climb up there?"

"Of course," Cass replied confidently, forgetting that she was wearing a long silk dress, borrowed from a begrudging Ornella. But she couldn't go and change, so, attracting some strange looks from the guests who noticed her, she hoiked up the dress and began to climb as best she could. "He'd better be here," she muttered to herself, pulling herself up the wooden rungs, her arms burning with the effort.

He was there. He stood with his back to her, silhouetted against the night sky.

"Rip," she panted, as she reached the top of the ladder. "Your uncle wants you."

Getting into the crow's nest was difficult at the best of times, as you had to haul yourself up on to the platform, but it was virtually impossible for Cass without ruining the dress. Before she could even try to attempt it, Rip came over, and taking both her hands, pulled her in.

"I'm sorry you had to climb up to get me in that dress," he said, smiling at her. "Though it does look very pretty on you," he added hastily.

How nice it is up here, Cass thought as she looked around, taking in the pile of cushions and books. They were so high in the sky that the stars seemed to wrap around them like a tent, and the noise and the chatter of the party sounded miles below.

"It's my hideaway," Rip said, reading her thoughts. "How's the party? The same as all the others?"

Cass laughed, saying, "I don't know, I've only been to a few."

"Take it from me, they are all the same," said Rip. "An expensive waste of silvers that my uncle does not have. I cannot wait to be of age in six months' time and leave," he added with a bitterness that Cass had never heard him express before.

"Where will you go?" she asked, surprised by his tone as well as the idea that anyone could ever want to leave somewhere as fun and luxurious as the Palace Ship.

"Perhaps to the Far Isles, or I'd love to see Pingquing. It's pretty easy to pick up work as a navigator," he replied, his tone changing back to normal.

"We should get back to the party," Cass said.

"A few more minutes won't make any difference. Come and look at the view," Rip said.

Cass stood next to him, looking far out over the

little port at the other boats and the quayside.

"It's excellent for spying on people," she announced. "Because you are so high up, you really can see everything."

"I know," Rip replied with a laugh.

He bent down, picked up a bottle of flower beer and uncorked it, offering it to Cass. She took it gratefully and had a long swig, before handing it back.

"You can see right into those buildings," she exclaimed, pointing to a row of houses on the harbour. "Look there, at that family having dinner together. How nice. What do you think they are eating?"

"Well, they all look very happy so perhaps something delicious like crabfish fritters," Rip replied.

"Yum, lucky them, I love those too," Cass said, warming to her game. "Look at that mother putting her baby to bed in the house next door," she said, and then regretted it as they both fell quiet for a moment thinking of their own lost mothers, as they watched the woman tenderly kiss the child.

Lightening the mood, Rip said, "Do you see those children down there?" He leaned into her, pointing to a gang of children sitting on a bench on the quayside. "I wonder what they are plotting?"

Cass giggled, following his gaze, and instinctively leaning slightly back against him.

"Some wickedness I should think. At home in Minaris, my friend Tig and I used to peer in at the windows of the rich merchants' houses when they were having parties. One day, we obviously spent too long peering in, because one of the servants came out and shooed us away."

Rip laughed and turned to gaze back at the sea.

"Look at this," he said, taking Cass's hand to pull her over to the other side of the crow's nest. In the water to one side of the ship was a moving, glowing silver shape. It undulated through the sea, dissolving and then coming together again in a different form. It was one of the strangest and most beautiful things Cass had ever seen.

"What is it?" she asked.

"The naturalists say that the sea is full of tiny creatures too small for us to see, which give off light, like fireflies, when something stirs them up. There must be a shoal of fish swimming through the water there," he explained.

"That's amazing," Cass said, looking at the twisting silver shape, happily aware of Rip's solid presence next to her and his hand in hers.

They stood there together for a moment in perfect silence and stillness. It was just a moment, and at the time Cass thought little of it. But, with everything that was to happen afterwards, she would remember it for her whole life.

A shout from below broke the spell.

Cass dropped Rip's hand, suddenly embarrassed. "We'd better go down," she said.

Rip paused, looking at her, and then inclined his head in a nod. He followed her silently as she struggled clumsily down the rope ladder.

Later that evening, just as the party was finishing, Bastien came over to Cass.

"Are you enjoying life on my ship?" he asked, waving his cigarillo in the air.

"Yes, sire," she replied with a smile. How could she not?

"I'm so pleased," he replied. He looked like he was just going to wish her goodnight, but then he paused, saying, "If I might ask you a small favour then?"

"Yes of course, anything," Cass replied politely.

"Would you be so kind as to help Enzo with something that he's doing for me tomorrow night in Marma? He will explain more then."

It sounded harmless enough, and as Cass felt she owed Bastien so much, she assured him that she would. And then they wished each other goodnight.

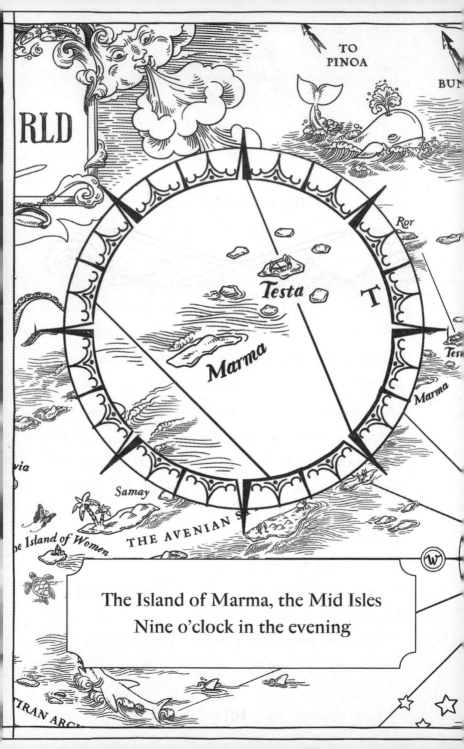

The Island of Marma, the Mid Isles
Nine o'clock in the evening

VII

Thief in the Night

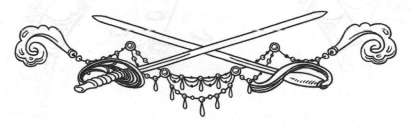

It was a beautiful evening and the Palace Ship was moored in a perfect little cove. A cascade of white rocks and pine forests poured down steep hillsides into a bay of blue-green sea. Enzo rowed Cass not to the little beach as she was expecting but round several rocky headlands. Dusk settled over them but the light was still clear enough to see another small beach and some way above it, nestled in the trees, a large mansion. A few lights from it flickered erratically through the trees.

"Is that where we are going?" Cass whispered.

Enzo nodded, not offering any more information.

She had asked him before what they were doing, and he had told her firmly to wait and see.

The beach was sandy and they pulled the boat up on to it noiselessly. Enzo slung two empty canvas bags over his shoulder and led them up the narrow overgrown stairs to the house. Cass could see that they had once been grand but the marble slabs had buckled and moved around, and plants had sprouted up between them. At last they reached an immense old iron gate, orange with rust. Cass was about to push it open but Enzo stopped her.

"It will make a terrible noise," he warned to Cass's puzzlement and instead he led them along the high wall that surrounded the house, looking for a break in it. Sure enough they hadn't walked far when they found a collapsed section. They scrambled over it easily.

"Please tell me what's going on," she urged Enzo. All the sneaking about was making her nervous.

But he simply replied that she would see soon enough.

Below the house, what had once been terraces

of ornamental gardens had been turned into vegetable plots. Enzo led Cass through the rows of salad and bashed old fruit cages, staying out of sight of the house above. Cass could hear chickens nearby, in a great clatter about something, and their wire enclosure soon came into view. In it stood two people. Even from a distance Cass could clearly see that they were elderly; the man was stooped right over his walking stick. The woman looked more sprightly. She was feeding the chickens, moving to and fro, throwing them their feed, almost as if she were dancing for them. As Cass and Enzo moved closer, they could hear her singing to them, above the din of squawking.

When the feeding was finished, the couple locked up the enclosure and then walked hand in hand back to the house. *How sweet!* Cass thought.

"Look, the last descendant of the greatest family of the Mid Isles, a mad chicken lady," Enzo mocked. "But a mad chicken lady with a very fine collection of jewels and a great store of silvers by all accounts."

"Why do you care about her jewels and silvers?" Cass asked him, bewildered.

"Because I like to be properly rewarded for my efforts," Enzo replied.

Cass was about to ask him what in the Longest World he was talking about when a horrible thought struck her.

"Are you going to rob these people?" she gasped.

Enzo raised an eyebrow, saying, "It's a little late for a picnic."

"But … but…" Cass let out a horrified splutter. "Why do you need to rob them? Surely you have enough money. Your father is Lord Protector of the Islands…"

Enzo cut her off, his face hard. "My father is entirely broke – he has spent all his money, and Lycus and the money lenders will give him no more. So this is how we survive."

Cass was so shocked that she couldn't speak.

"And I was rather hoping that you were going to help me, Cass," Enzo continued. "You see, I have been looking for an assistant for a while; someone agile and quick. You are perfect for the job."

When Cass didn't reply immediately, he added, "I don't doubt you make an excellent social secretary too."

Cass ignored him, asking instead, "What about Rip or Ornella? Why don't they help you?"

"Ornella is too clumsy and Rip has too many principles," he replied, with an edge to his voice.

"What makes you think I don't have principles?" Cass snapped.

Enzo paused before calmly replying, "I am sure you do. But you want my father to speak to Ravellous, don't you?"

Cass swallowed, suddenly and devastatingly aware of the real reason that Bastien had invited her to travel with them and the bargain she seemed to have entered into without knowing. She remembered Elsba's words: *Lord Bastien is not known for his kindness – he mostly does things that profit himself.*

"This may sound an obvious thing to point out but I just want to make sure matters are absolutely clear to you," Enzo went on. "As I think I've established, my father and I have no principles. But if you refuse to help, you will be staying on Marma with the chicken lady. I believe the mail boat visits here every two weeks. You might be able to catch a ride back to Testa, and there I suppose you could pick up another ship going to the Island of Women, but do you have the silvers to pay for another passage?"

Cass tried to digest all that Enzo had said. The kaleidoscope of her world had turned and an entirely new, unpleasant pattern had been revealed. It took Cass some moments to adjust to the reality of her situation and when she did, she had to acknowledge that Enzo was right; she only had a few silvers left, not nearly enough to pay for another passage. She had been entirely cornered.

"So will you help me?" he asked.

"It doesn't appear I have much option, does it?" Cass replied coldly.

"Not really, no," Enzo admitted. "But good. I am pleased, even if you're not."

"You won't hurt them, the chicken lady and her husband, will you?" Cass asked.

"No," Enzo replied emphatically. "That I can promise you. So to business. We will wait for them to go to bed and fall asleep." He crouched down behind a bush, scanning the house, working out its layout.

Cass looked at the house too. It had clearly once been a magnificent mansion but now it was horribly neglected. Nature was slowly reclaiming the house for itself, strangling it with vines and creepers. The ground-floor windows were shuttered but the upstairs ones were open, allowing Enzo and Cass to glimpse the couple progressing along the corridor to their bedrooms, the orange flames of their candles bobbing along. The lights stayed on in two of the upper rooms for a while and then went out.

"When I see the first star we will go," Enzo said, lying back on the hard baked earth so he could stare at the evening sky.

"Won't they wake up?" Cass asked.

"No, the best time to rob people is in the first hours after they fall asleep. It is then that you are most deeply asleep."

I really don't want to do this, Cass thought, but there was no way out of it that she could see.

Ten minutes later, Enzo sat up, pointing at a

pinprick of white light above the house. The first star. They walked quietly up to the house.

Enzo pulled at a loose shutter on the ground floor. Cass had expected to see a window behind it, but they were long gone, leaving nothing but a gaping hole. So they simply climbed over the windowsill. Enzo handed her one of the canvas bags.

"Put anything you are sure is valuable in this. If you don't know ask me," he instructed in a whisper. "There's no hurry so we'll start down here." He produced a couple of candles in metal holders, which he lit, giving her one.

Cass found the house intensely creepy and all her instincts were telling her to get out of there immediately. It was filthy and the ceilings had collapsed in several rooms, leaving messy piles of plaster and wood. There were insects everywhere; huge fluttering moths bashed into her, attracted by the candle flame, giant, feathery centipedes darted along the walls and beetles carpeted the floor, crunching under her shoes. Several snakes slithered away from her, making her spring back in revulsion. There were even bats roosting in the ceiling of one room. But none of it seemed to bother Enzo in the slightest. He wandered through the rooms leisurely, picking up objects and then, as often as not, discarding them unless they were silver or gold. These he placed in his bag.

They must have been in the house for at least half an hour before they finally walked out into a huge hall, where a grand stone staircase wound its way up to the first floor. It was lit by what must have been a huge glass roof light, but the glass was lost and there was only sky above them. There was no need for candles so they blew them out. Enzo gestured for Casss to leave her bag at the top of the stairs.

"We mustn't risk waking them without finding the money and jewellery," Enzo whispered. "So let's go to their bedrooms first, which are those two rooms there. You take the first and I will take the second. Remember the man will probably have the money and the woman the jewels. Look under the bed."

The door was ajar and Cass walked tentatively inside. In contrast to the rest of the house the room was practically empty and the walls had been newly whitewashed. The moonlight poured in through the open window, illuminating the figure of the woman lying on her side with her back to Cass in a canopied four-poster bed. By the window was a table and Cass tiptoed over to it. A few pieces of jewellery lay on a tray and Cass pocketed them. There was also a box. It didn't look like a coin chest but Cass gently opened it. It was full of letters so she shut it again, letting the lid fall too quickly. She held her breath as she heard the woman stir. *Please don't wake up*, Cass prayed. The woman turned over on to her other side and her breathing returned to normal.

Cass desperately wanted to leave, but she knew that Enzo would not be satisfied with the jewellery she had found, and would send her back. She looked around the room. There was only a clothes stand with some tatty dresses draped over it and a small bookshelf. The books appeared very ordinary ones to Cass. She should look under the bed, she thought, as Enzo had told her to.

Cass knelt down, lifting the heavy valance, which sent up so much dust that she struggled not to cough. She peered into the gloom. It took her eyes a few moments to adjust, but then she could see the outline of a box. It was in the middle and she had to wriggle right under the bed to reach it. It was difficult but at last she got it, and pulling it out, emerged from under the bed with it in her hands.

"Who are you?"

Cass nearly dropped the box with fright. The old lady was sitting up in bed, her face turned towards Cass with a puzzled expression on her face.

"Who are you?" she repeated in a querulous tone. "Answer me! Are you one of the new servant girls?"

"Yes," Cass replied, edging towards the door. "I'm a new servant girl and I'm very sorry to disturb you."

The old lady looked appeased.

"Well, next time you want to clean under my bed, don't do it in the middle of the night. Otherwise I will tell Mama and you will lose your job. Now leave me to sleep. I have a very exhausting day tomorrow – it's my birthday and there will be a picnic and a trip to the waterfall and…"

Cass, her heart beating and drenched in sweat, began to back out of the room, the box in her hand.

"But where are you taking my box?" the old lady demanded.

"Oh, just to clean it," Cass found herself replying.

The old lady looked at her for a long moment.

"I don't think you are a maid at all," she said pausing and then shrieked, "I think you're a thief!" And like an ancient cat, she sprang out of bed and lunged at Cass.

But Cass was younger and faster. She ran out of the room and down the stairs to find Enzo waiting for her, holding the bags. She turned to see the old lady at the top of the stairs, like a ghost in her white nightgown.

"Stop, thief in the night! Stop, thief in the night!" the old woman's voice rose behind them like a siren.

They ran out of the house and down the steps, not stopping until they had stumbled and tripped their way down to the beach.

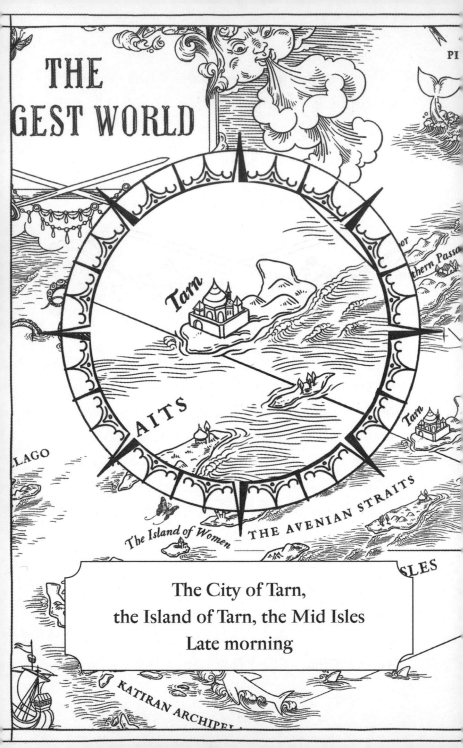

THE
GEST WORLD

Tarn

AITS

Tarn

LAGO

Northern Passa

The Island of Women   THE AVENIAN STRAITS

SLES

KATIRAN ARCHIPEL

The City of Tarn,
the Island of Tarn, the Mid Isles
Late morning

VIII

A Leopard at the Party

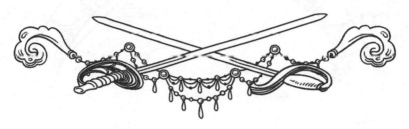

Tarn, the bohemian capital of the Mid Isles, was a shambolic jumble of houseboats and buildings sprawling out over the sheltered lagoon where it was situated. It was protected from the sea by a chain of small islands known collectively as the Necklace of Tarn. It was a city that deeply divided opinion; some adored it – the energy, the carnival atmosphere, its crumbling beauty – while others hated it for the dirt, the beggars and the indifferent rich. There was a local saying that encapsulated it perfectly – *in Tarn do you smell the jasmine or the rubbish?*

As the Palace Ship sailed into the harbour,

cutting a stately path through the tangle of slavers' ships, fishing boats and merchants' schooners, Cass felt her spirits lift a little. She spied the Circus Boat moored on the other side and allowed herself to think that in just a few days' time it might be her new home. For despite its luxury, the Palace Ship had now become for Cass the most wretched place in the Longest World. Since robbing the elderly couple, she had stayed in her cabin as much as she could, avoiding Bastien and Enzo. She found herself shunning Rip too, for she felt so ashamed for having been involved with the thieving, even though Enzo had left her little choice. She couldn't wait to leave the ship, so when Ornella announced that she was busy that morning visiting her cousin, Cass leaped at the opportunity to explore Tarn. But Tarn was quite a shock to Cass. Used to the orderly hustle and bustle of stately Minaris, Cass found Tarn chaotic and alarming. She hated the strong smell of the harbour for a start. It was a mix of the filthy water, dirt, tar and fish. And she couldn't bear all the people jostling her – their constant shouting and the noise jangled her nerves. Beggar children came whining and pulling at her clothes, hassling her for silvers which upset her, as did the sight of slaves – chained men and women shuffling miserably along, pushing carts or carrying heavy loads. She found it all so overwhelming that she was about to give up and go back to the ship, when she heard someone call her name.

Rip appeared by her side.

"I haven't seen you for a while. Where are you off to?" he asked.

Cass hesitated because she had intended to avoid Rip. But then seeing him was such a relief and made her feel so instantly better that she found herself telling him that she was going to explore the city.

"Do you mind if I join you?" he asked. "There's not much for a navigator to do on a moored ship and it is far too nice a day to spend it reading a book in my cabin."

"Of course, I'd really like that," Cass replied, smiling for the first time in days.

"Good," he said, looking equally pleased. He immediately distributed a good amount of coins to the beggar children on the condition that they leave them alone, and then led Cass away from the harbour and up the narrow streets that led to the famous Square of Obfuscation and Tower of Seven Kingdoms.

The square was quite unlike anything Cass had ever come across before. The squares in Minaris were large and elegant and most of all empty, whereas the Square of Obfuscation was crammed with a disordered stew of food sellers, fortune tellers, storytellers, snake charmers, ice stalls, makeshift inns, booksellers, street artists, night ladies and pretty much anything else you can imagine.

"Hold on to your purse," Rip instructed as they made their way into it, taking her hand so they didn't get separated by the crowds.

It was amazing and exhausting, so after an hour or so of roaming around and admiring the Tower with its intricate carved stonework, they bought starfruit ice cones from a stall and they wandered down an alley, picking their way through the maze of streets. The city became quieter and Cass could catch glimpses of cool courtyards hidden behind the brightly painted wooden doors that lined the streets.

Rip stopped at a large stone arched doorway,

with an inscription written above it and the carving of a woman's face.

"This is Mele's house – how funny. I have always wanted to visit here and have looked for it several times and never found it. Do you mind if we go in? "

Cass nodded, trying to remember who Mele was – she definitely knew the name from somewhere but couldn't think why.

They walked into a large courtyard with an ancient mulberry tree in the middle. There were several people sitting in its shade, drinking bitter tea, and one of them, an elderly lady, got to her feet, calling out to them.

"Welcome to the house of Mele! Let me tell you a little about her and then I can show you the tomb."

They thanked the lady, who began her tour.

"Mele was born eighty-three years ago here in Tarn and she was one of the greatest sword fighters who ever lived, man or woman. She played a crucial role in the Magical Wars, killing the Grand Mage Titus."

Oh yes of course, Cass thought. *I remember now.*

Madame Carpera mentioned her.

"As you may know," the lady continued, "she was an obtuse, which made it possible for her to kill some great magicians, as she was virtually immune to their magic."

"I told you it was a gift," Rip whispered to Cass. "Mele was also a strict adherent to her famous *Code for an Honourable Life* and, after the wars, she devoted her time to helping the people of Tarn and the Islands."

The lady led Cass and Rip up a steep flight of steps and into a large circular room lined with stone carvings and a roof made of glass bullseyes. A stone bench was in the middle and Cass and the guide sat down on it as they looked around the room.

"Mele's ashes are buried all around the room in those small round brass caskets you can see set into the stone, so she remains everywhere, which was what she wanted. And the sculptures depict her life – there you can see her as a baby and then a young girl growing up in Tarn, and then fighting her first sword fights. And this is Mele in the Magical Wars, riding her white horse into battle… And look, that is her with her other sword fighters." She paused, pointing at a collection of other women flanking Mele, all dressed in breeches and holding swords up in a salute to her. "I am afraid I cannot name them all, but overall they were known as Mele's Sword Fighters or the Company of Eight.

"The Company still survives today, helping those in need and vanquishing evil, as they did in Mele's time, but these days, it has become an underground organization and the identity of its eight members is a closely guarded secret. And finally look at this last picture of Mele in her old age, surrounded by the people of Tarn," the guide said, finishing her tour.

Cass and Rip gave the lady a few silvers for her trouble and made their way back out into the street.

"Enzo and I always tease Idaliz about being a member of the Company of Eight, although obviously she will never admit it," Rip said.

Cass laughed. "Lucky her if she is. I would love to be able to fight like Idaliz," she said, remembering the swordfighting lesson. And then she thought of Elsba too, and said to Rip, "I met another woman who was also an amazing fighter. Without a weapon, she chased off two thieves who attacked me in Loutrekia…" And then Cass stopped still, her mouth dropping open in amazement as she remembered the eight tattoo on Elsba's back she had glimpsed at the baths.

"What is it?" Rip asked.

Cass smiled to herself, thinking she had better keep Elsba's secret safe. "Nothing," she said. "I'm starving. Would you like something to eat?"

They found an inn tucked away down an alley, with a pretty, shady garden that sold crabfish fritters. They sat eating plates of them and drinking flower beer while they chatted away, as the afternoon drifted on into the evening. Cass was having such a nice time that she had forgotten all about the robbing.

Eventually they made their way back along the quay where a crowd had gathered in front of the Circus Boat, watching as a few performers put on a street show to drum up customers for the tent shows that were to begin the following day. Cass recognized Wildo the juggler, who was sending green glass globes spinning through the air, and there were a couple of acrobats doing tricks together. But, as ever, the main attraction was Helene and her act on a thick silk ribbon. The circusters had rigged it up to a frame and she was making the crowds gasp as she worked her way up and down, twirling and dangling, as the orchestra played a mournful tune. Ravellous the Circus Master was standing nearby, watching her and the crowd's reaction.

Cass stopped to gaze in admiration, feeling the familiar shivers of excitement. There was still nothing she wanted more than to be a part of it. Would Bastien keep his word? she wondered. Perhaps she should go to speak to Ravellous herself and explain about missing the audition.

But before she could decide, the harbour clock rang out the hour and Rip said reluctantly, "I think we had better go, otherwise we'll be late for tonight's party."

Cass nodded, thinking that she would remind Bastien of his side of the bargain. She had kept hers after all.

"Where have you been? You're not even changed and people are about to arrive!" Ornella shouted at Cass when she walked into the cabin. Cass muttered an apology and quickly pulled on her dress and tidied her hair.

The party began as they always did with a trickle of people that turned into a steady stream, and soon the deck was crowded and Cass had to weave carefully between everyone, escorting people over to Bastien. She wanted to ask him if he had spoken to Ravellous but he was never free.

Cass returned to Ornella after one such trip to be greeted by the most extraordinary sight. Ornella was speaking to a woman who was remarkably beautiful, and exquisitely dressed in a long white silk dress, with an ornate gold, pearl and emerald necklace round her neck. But none of that made any impression on Cass as she was far too busy looking at the leopard sitting calmly by the woman's side, a collar round his neck attached to a chain that the woman held casually in her hand. She had only seen such creatures in pictures before and was captivated. It was smaller than she'd imagined but its teeth looked as sharp as needles.

Ornella clearly knew the woman, and as Cass approached she said, "Cass, this is my cousin, Narina. Cass is my helper. She will take you to Bastien if you want."

"Not necessary," the woman replied with a smirk.

Cass couldn't resist putting her hand out to touch the leopard, as she asked, "Is he friendly?"

The woman laughed as the leopard lunged at Cass's hand. She jerked it back just in time.

"No, my dear, he is a wild animal not a cat." And she sauntered over the deck, the crowds parting to let her through. Bastien came forward.

"Narina," he greeted her expansively, kissing both her hands, his gaze resting a little too long on her necklace.

Cass then watched Enzo bow to Narina. He too was unable to keep his eyes off the jewels. *Oh no, not again*, Cass thought, trying to quell the feeling of dread gripping her throat.

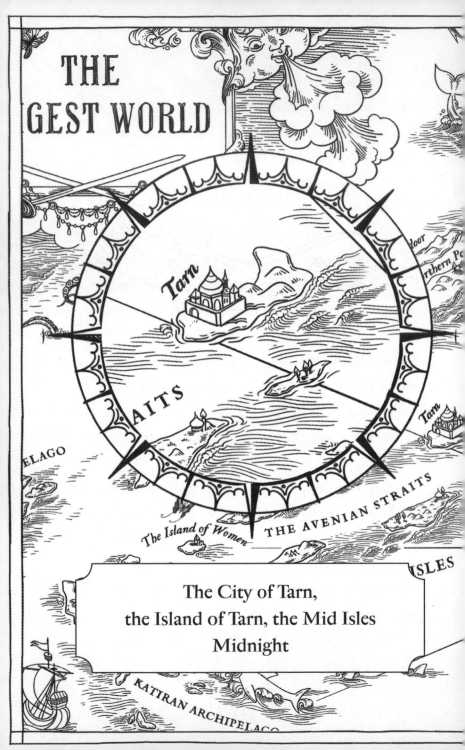

THE
~~GEST WORLD~~

Tarn

AITS

Tarn

ELAGO

The Island of Women   THE AVENIAN STRAITS

~~door~~
~~rthern P~~

~~ISLES~~

The City of Tarn,
the Island of Tarn, the Mid Isles
Midnight

KATIRAN ARCHIPELAGO

IX

A Trip to Narina's Houseboat

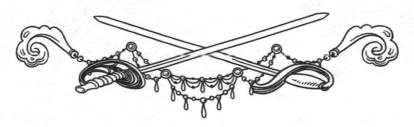

Cass and Ornella were both fast asleep when Enzo came into the cabin as quietly as a cat. He put his hand on Cass's arm and shook her awake.

"It's time to get dressed," he whispered.

It was just as Cass had feared. "Do I have to come?" she asked wearily.

"You do indeed. I need your help reeling in that incredibly ostentatious necklace that Narina was showing off tonight," he replied. "And presumably you want my father to speak to Ravellous tomorrow."

Cass tipped herself reluctantly out of the hammock and pulled on her clothes.

Narina lived on a houseboat, an old barge built in the style typical of Tarn, with elaborate carved woodwork picked out in silver paint. The grander the houseboat, the more isolated it was, and Narina's was tethered to its own pier.

Enzo rowed them beyond it so they could get a good look. The pier was all lit up with lanterns and there were a gaggle of watchmen sitting cross-legged, smoking.

"There is no way of getting past them unseen," Enzo whispered to Cass and rowed the boat out in a broad sweep around the houseboat to see if they could get to it from the lagoon side.

There were no other boats in sight and no sign of watchmen on board, so Enzo brought the rowing boat nearer to the barge to have a closer inspection. He knew from having been to the barge with his father that Narina's bedroom and dressing room lay at the rear.

There were only two ways to get into them – either by the door that led from the front of the barge or by climbing in through one of the round windows that gave on to the rooms.

Enzo studied the windows carefully. It was a hot

airless night, so they were open but they were high up, in a sheer wall with only a narrow ledge at the water level beneath. He couldn't use a grappling hook and rope – the noise would be sure to wake Narina.

The only way would be for him to lift Cass up and then she could pull herself through.

Enzo asked Cass whether she could do it.

She answered his question with another. "Where's the leopard?"

"Oh, it will be keeping guard at the front of the barge," he replied confidently and as if in answer, they heard a muffled roar. It did sound to Cass like it was some distance away.

"So, can you do it, Cass?" Enzo asked.

Not one bit of Cass wanted to crawl through the window on to the houseboat and search through someone's belongings for a necklace, but every bit of her desperately wanted to leave the Palace Ship and get on to the Circus Boat. She saw clearly that one was not going to happen without the other so she replied curtly to Enzo, "Yes."

Enzo brought the boat close in. There was nowhere to moor it but Cass gestured for him to bend over and hold on to the ledge. He did as she said, and she climbed up his bent back as nimbly as if he were a staircase before silently pulling herself across to the high window. She rested on the sill, half in and half out, gracefully balancing.

Enzo was right and it was indeed Narina's dressing room, which was in a terrible mess. It was very dark but Cass could make out clothes strewn everywhere and on the other side of the room was a table crowded with bottles and boxes and trays of glittering jewellery. A door was half open to the bedroom beyond, revealing a slice of black quiet, with only the faint sound of breathing audible.

Cass looked around nervously for the leopard, but there was no sign of it. She was relieved to see a sofa right below the window that she could easily vault down on to and which would enable an easy escape once she was finished. Feeling confident, she slithered down into the room.

The necklace, Cass reasoned, was most likely to be on the table, so that was where she looked first. But she could still hardly believe her eyes when it was actually there, lying curled up like a little snake. She picked it up silently and examined it, the stones shimmering darkly.

As she was about to slip it into her pocket, she heard a slight noise behind her. *Oh no*, Cass thought, *not the leopard!* But then she felt something cold and hard shoved against her throat and her arms were pinned behind her back in one swift and painful movement. She dropped the necklace.

"What do you think you're doing?" said a male voice, quiet and smooth with a trace of a Far Isles accent. He yanked her arms further and painfully up her back, while pressing the flat side of a knife hard into her windpipe.

In that moment, Cass realized she had never in her life been properly frightened. But she was now. Her whole world became reduced to the pain in her arms and neck and the liquid fear in her stomach.

Someone else walked into the room with a candle, and the man swung Cass around to face them.

It was Narina dressed in a silk wrap, her face sleepy.

"Look what I found in your dressing room," the

man said. "A little thief. Your necklace is on the floor. Shall I kill her?"

Cass's heart was thumping so loudly with fear that she couldn't understand how it hadn't burst.

Narina picked up the necklace, and after checking it wasn't damaged, returned it to the table. Then she looked at Cass, regarding her for a long moment. *Please don't recognize me*, Cass prayed.

"I know you," Narina said at last. "You were helping Ornella on Bastien's boat this evening. Remind me of your name?"

"Cassandra," Cass managed to reply.

"Did Bastien send you?" Narina asked, her eyes narrowing.

"No," Cass said, shaking her head furiously.

"Then who did?" the man asked, his voice loud in her ear.

"No one sent me, I came on my own," Cass replied.

Narina walked over to the window and looked out.

"No one else is there now, but I don't believe you. How did you get here?"

"Along the jetty," Cass answered, without thinking it through.

"What, past the watchmen and my leopard? I don't think so," Narina replied.

The man pulled Cass's arms harder, making her gasp in pain, and tears flooded her eyes.

"I think we need to pay Bastien a little visit," the man said. "I've been looking forward to meeting him anyway."

"I agree," said Narina. "Wait a moment while I dress." She disappeared back into her bedroom with a handful of clothes.

The man released Cass and she heard him pulling on some clothes behind her but she did not move a muscle. Once he was dressed, he tied her wrists behind her so tightly that her hands tingled. But she didn't dare complain – her brain felt as if it were locked in one thought, which was simply, *Please don't kill me.*

Afterwards, Cass remembered little of the walk

back to Bastien's ship – just the mind-numbing fear, and the excruciating pain in her wrists and hands. They were accompanied by a number of the watchmen, but they were behind Cass, as was her captor, who pushed her ahead of him so she still hadn't seen his face.

The deck of the Palace Ship was quiet, but one of the watchmen scampered off to tell Bastien of their arrival and they were escorted down to his chambers speedily.

He was with Ornella, and their expressions were serious but not unduly alarmed, Cass thought. She guessed Enzo had told them what had happened and she allowed herself a glimmer of hope that everything would be all right.

Cass was released by her captor, and for the first time she could have a proper look at him. He was a good-looking Far Islander, about forty years old, with thick dark curly hair swept off his face, and a beard. He wore glasses, which gave him a studious look and if Cass had met him under different circumstances, she would have taken him for an apothecary or an academic.

They both came forward to be introduced.

"This is Varen," Narina said, with just a hint of a challenge in her eyes and a smile about her lips. Cass could see her waiting to see Bastien's reaction.

The name meant nothing to Cass, nor Ornella, Cass noticed, but it seemed to mean a good deal to Bastien for he paled and licked his lips, running his fingers through his hair.

"I have heard much about you," he replied, offering his hand.

"And I have heard much about you too," Varen replied calmly. "I am sorry we have to meet under such unfortunate circumstances," he went on, taking charge of the situation. "I caught this girl –" he gestured to Cass – "stealing from Narina. She was in her dressing room, with the necklace in her hand. I understand she works for you."

"Not as a thief, she doesn't. And it is only a casual arrangement," Bastien replied quickly. "I am absolutely horrified, and can only apologize. I will deal with her in the strongest terms."

Let that be the end of it, Cass prayed.

Varen paused before saying, in the mildest tone of voice, "If you don't mind, I would like to deal with her myself."

"Of course, the girl is yours if you wish," Bastien replied. "Come, let us have a drink and try to repair some of the damage that has been done by us meeting under such circumstances. I will get someone to guard her while we talk. I am sure there is much to discuss that we do not need an audience for."

"I prefer that one of my men guard her," Varen said, again in a voice as neutral as if he were discussing the weather.

"As you wish," Bastien replied. "Ornella, please take Cass to your room, tie her up, lock her in and then fetch one of Varen's men from the deck."

"Of course," Ornella agreed and she hauled Cass out of the room. The door was shut firmly behind them.

Enzo was lurking outside the door, his face anxious. He grabbed Cass by the elbow sharply, saying, "You haven't told them about me, have you?"

"No," Cass replied.

"Good," he said and released her. "Well, don't. I can't believe you were so stupid as to get caught."

"It wasn't my fault," she protested, her voice

cracking with the strain.

"Of course it was. You must have made too much noise," Enzo hissed, looking at her as if she were a worm that he had found in his food. "So what is to be done with her?" he asked Ornella.

"I am to guard her until they have finished talking. Then Narina's boyfriend will punish her."

Enzo shrugged. "He probably just wants to slap you around to look manly in front of Narina. Right, I'm going to get some sleep now." And without another word to Cass, he turned on his heels and left.

"Come on," Ornella said, with a note of kindness in her voice Cass didn't expect. She led her to their room.

Cass was too shocked to cry. She was mute and passive as a doll as Ornella tied her to a chair.

"What's going on?" a voice asked, and Cass glanced up to see Rip. She immediately looked away, mortified.

"She has been caught stealing from Narina by her boyfriend. I have to go and fetch one of his men to guard her now while they talk to your uncle," Ornella explained with a sigh.

Rip looked at Cass with amazement. "With Enzo?" he asked, and then when she didn't reply he asked her again, more insistently, "Were you with Enzo?"

Cass nodded guiltily.

"But he wasn't caught?" Rip questioned.

Cass shook her head.

"Was it the first time?" he asked.

Cass shook her head and said, staring at the floor, unable to look at Rip, "No, I went with him in Marma. He made it very clear it was why I was here on the boat and that I would be left there if I didn't help him."

"Who is Narina's boyfriend?" Rip asked Ornella.

"His name is Varen and I imagine he's a rich merchant," Ornella replied with a shrug.

Rip's face was a mirror to Bastien's reaction before.

"You're joking?" he said in a deadly serious voice and when Ornella looked puzzled he went on, "Varen is no merchant. He's the pirate chief!"

Cass thought she might be sick. "But he's going to take me, what will he do?" she cried.

"Hush," Rip snapped, fear for her making him

angry. Then after a moment, "We have to get you off the boat."

Rip looked at the small window. "You will have to swim," he said to Cass. "You must let her go, Ornella."

"And get into trouble with the pirates myself?" she said. "No, absolutely not. I feel sorry for Cass, but I can't do that."

"Narina is your cousin – she won't let anything bad happen to you. Besides, we can make it look like someone broke in and overpowered you. They must suspect you were working with someone else?" he asked Cass, who nodded.

"I won't do it," Ornella insisted.

"Have a heart, Ornella. Think what the pirates will do to her," said Rip.

Ornella swallowed and looked away.

"You had better make it look good then," she replied. "You'll need to tie me up and mess up the room as if there was a struggle. And hurry because I am supposed to have fetched one of his men by now."

"Oh, thank you, Ornella. Thank you so much," Cass gushed, wiping away her tears. She felt some hope trickle back as Rip deftly untied the knots, allowing her to stand.

Ornella took her place and let Rip tie her up.

"You need to hit me too," Ornella said.

"Really?" Rip asked.

"Yes, then it can look like you knocked me out. Gag me first," she said.

Rip nodded, getting a handkerchief out of his pocket and gagging her as loosely as he could. And then Cass looked away as he punched Ornella. Her face contorted in pain as a livid red mark sprung up on her face.

Rip opened the small window and helped Cass out of it, lowering her down to the sea so she could get in as silently as possible.

They had agreed that she would swim around to the steps at the far end of the quay and he would meet her there.

The sun had risen and the dock was coming to life, with fishermen unloading their night's work. Cass swam away from the ship, diving right down into the filthy water to avoid being seen from the deck. She only let herself surface when she was some distance away. She swam to the steps and got out of the water as unobtrusively as possible.

Rip was waiting for her, and they darted into a quiet passage where they tried to wring as much water out of Cass's clothes and hair as possible.

"You need to get far away from the harbour, and stay away from it," Rip said.

Cass nodded, too petrified to speak. She couldn't get the sensation of Varen holding the knife to her throat out of her mind.

"I think it is best you go back to Mele's house and stay there. I'll come and find you later," Rip said. "Do you remember the way?"

Cass nodded.

"Good," he replied, fishing a small bag of coins from his pocket. "Here are a few silvers so you can eat and stay in a lodging house tonight in case I can't leave the ship – leave word for me of where you've gone with the guide there. I'll bring more silvers when I return and we can make a plan."

Cass wanted to grab him by the arm and beg him to stay with her, not to leave her alone in this strange city where she knew no one, with the threat of being pursued by pirates.

But she didn't, she just mumbled, "You will

come back, won't you?"

"Of course," he assured her.

"You and Ornella must not take any blame for what has happened," Cass went on. "I'm so sorry I got caught."

"It wasn't your fault, Cass," Rip replied kindly. "They should never have involved you." He took her hand gently in his. "Everything will be fine, I'm sure. Just be sensible and stay hidden. Now I must go and so must you. Be safe until we meet again."

And he walked briskly back to the quay.

Cass did as Rip said and made her way to Mele's house, choosing the narrowest, quietest lanes, nervously glancing behind her constantly. When at last she reached it, the gate was shut, for it was still very early.

So she found a quiet corner and sat down, shivering in her damp clothes and quietly put her head in her hands and wept, like she hadn't since she was a little girl. She cried at having been caught by the pirates, for Rip's kindness and for having been so stupid as to trust Bastien and Enzo.

"Why are you crying?' a voice asked and Cass raised her head to see a girl standing above her. She was in her late teens, and had some of Tig's scragginess combined with the dark skin of a Mid Islander, and the bluest eyes that Cass had ever seen. They looked like coloured glass. She was dressed in a riot of pink and purple silks, with gold rings in her ears and on her hands.

Cass wanted to ignore her but there was an insistence to the girl's stare that slightly intimidated her, so she just muttered, "No reason," in reply, wiping away her tears.

"Do you live around here?" the girl asked.

Cass shook her head.

"Where do you come from?"

"Loutrekia," Cass lied, blowing her nose on her sleeve.

"Really?" The girl sounded impressed. "You're a long way from home."

Cass nodded, feeling the tears welling up in her eyes again.

"Don't cry any more," the girl said matter-of-factly. "Are you waiting for someone?"

Cass nodded, her brain springing into action.

"Yes, I'm meeting a friend but not until later this morning," she replied.

"Well, I can't leave you here looking so sad. Why don't you come back with me? I live just around the corner and I can make you some breakfast. It'll be nicer than sitting on a doorstep."

Cass weighed up her options. She felt acutely conspicuous on the street and the pirates could be combing the city for her at that moment. Surely she was safer inside a house? And this girl seemed nice.

Cass hesitated, unsure of what to do.

"It is really near," the girl said. "My name is Leila by the way. What's yours?"

"It's … Floss," she replied.

"Floss, that's a nice name," Leila said. "Well, Floss, come with me. I make very good cacao. It'll make all your troubles disappear!" And she held out her hand to Cass and pulled her up off the doorstep.

Leila's rooms were literally just around the corner, which reassured Cass, and were situated on the first floor of a large house.

"I live on my own. I'm an orphan," Leila

explained.

"Me too," said Cass.

The walls of Leila's room were painted bright pink, which seemed fabulously exotic to Cass – rooms in Minaris were never painted anything more daring than blue.

In the corner was a large birdcage full of canaries, which drew Cass like a magnet as soon as she walked in.

"They're so pretty," she cried, touching the bars of the cage, gazing at the bright yellow birds.

Leila laughed.

"Talk to them while I make the cacao. Or do you want to look at a book? I've got a few. Do you like to read?"

"Yes," Cass said.

"And do you like to write too?" Leila asked.

"Yes," Cass replied. "But I'd rather look at your birds."

Leila made herself busy at the tiny stove in the corner, heating up the water for cacao, her back to Cass.

"So who are you meeting?" Leila asked.

Cass hesitated. Nice as Leila seemed, she didn't

want to tell her too much.

"Just a friend."

Leila nodded sympathetically.

"Have you run away from somebody?" she asked. "Don't worry I won't tell anyone," she added when Cass didn't immediately reply.

"Sort of," Cass replied. She was beginning to find Leila's questions annoying.

"Here, drink this," Leila said, bringing over the cacao.

It was indeed hot, strong and very sweet and Cass drank it up greedily.

"More?" Leila asked.

"Yes please," Cass replied. Leila filled up her cup and gave her a sugar cake to eat with it too.

The sugar and the warmth of the cacao felt as if it were seeping into Cass's bones, relaxing her. She yawned widely and loudly.

Leila smiled.

"Why don't you lie down and have a nap?" she suggested. "My bed is through there. I'll wake you up in an hour or so and then you can go and meet your friend."

Cass accepted gratefully.

She lay down on the bed, which was solid and comforting after months of sleeping in hammocks, and fell instantly into a deep sleep.

THE
LONGEST WORLD

amay

Sedoor

the North

THE AVENIAN STRAITS

THE MID ISLES

CHIPELAGO

Tarn

The Island of Women   THE AVENIAN STRAITS

ISL

The Avenian Straits, twenty-five
nautical miles south-west of
the Island of Tarn, the Mid Isles
Dawn

KATIRAN AR

X

Goatsmilk

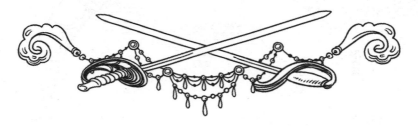

Cass woke up to the swaying of a moving boat and a terrible smell of sweat and dirt. Her brain felt so foggy and confused that it took a few seconds before she began to panic. The last thing that she remembered was lying down on Leila's bed, so why wasn't she there? Why was she lying on a thin mattress in the hold of a boat that smelled so awful? A terrible thought seized her brain. *The pirates must have found me somehow. Leila must have betrayed me to them.* She tried to sit up, but her hands and feet were bound, and her mouth was gagged. She struggled desperately and must have made some noise because a woman's voice came out of the dark, surprisingly close.

"Shut up!" it hissed in an island dialect that Cass could only just understand. "You'll get us all into trouble. Go back to sleep. It'll soon be morning."

Cass lay back, shot through with fear as her brain beat out its refrain, *Where am I? What has happened?*

"Get up!" A loud voice woke her and Cass felt herself being kicked. She opened her eyes to see a large, doughy-looking man, with cold, sharp black eyes like a raven, staring down at her. He looked like one of the wealthy spice merchants she had seen so often in Minaris and Cass's first thought was one of relief that at least he wasn't Varen and, at first glance, he didn't look like a pirate. Her next thought was that wherever she was, it was unspeakably hot and smelly. She sat up, her eyes darting quickly around her. She was in the hold of a medium-sized ship, which was empty apart from her. It was littered with soiled mattresses. Her mouth felt raw but her gag had been removed as well as the ropes around her hands and feet.

"Where am I and where's Leila?" Cass demanded.

"You are in the hold of my ship. And I should imagine Leila is buying herself a good deal of gold jewellery with the amount of silvers I just paid her for you."

Cass was baffled.

"I don't understand," she replied, getting to her feet. "What do you mean, paid for me? Who are you?"

"My name is Bang and I am one of the most successful slavers in the Mid Isles," he boasted.

"What am *I* doing on a slaving ship?" Cass asked, still bewildered.

The man burst out into horrible laughter.

"What do you think you're doing? We are on our way to the Great Slaver's Market at Riza and you will fetch me a pretty price. Leila said you can read and write."

"Yes, but I am not a slave! I am a free citizen of Minaris. I've just been on the Palace Ship for goodness' sake!" Cass's voice reached a crescendo, as she felt around her neck for the proof. "Where's my fish necklace?" she asked furiously. The purse Rip had given her had gone too. All that remained was the ring from Lin. Clearly it was too plain to have attracted Leila's attention.

"That's a pretty story, but I am not interested in it and neither will anyone in Riza. You are a very long way from Minaris here," he chuckled. "Leila sold you to me so you are now mine and soon you will belong to someone else. Now, do you want to come up on deck and have some fresh air and food?"

"I do not belong to you!" Cass shouted. "I demand that you release me and take me to shore."

The man's face hardened. "Make no mistake, girl, you do, and what's more you need to learn some manners." And to Cass's horrified amazement, he produced a cat-o'-nine-tails whip from his belt.

"Don't you dare strike me!" she shrieked. But Bang ignored her, and grabbed her arm.

"I am not some servant of yours to be ordered around. I am in charge here," he spat at her and before Cass knew what was happening he had hit her hard on her leg. The pain was excruciating and she had to clamp her mouth together to stop herself crying out.

"Next time it will be worse. Much worse. Now I don't really care whether you eat or not but there'll be no more food until sundown," he said as he stalked back up to the deck.

Cass slumped down on the mattress and examined the stinging trails of raw, bleeding skin that the whip had left, like a jellyfish's sting. Tears of fury slipped down her face. How dare he strike her. The other slaves came back down to the hold but she barely noticed them as she lay there, desperately wondering what to do.

The pain woke her again the following morning. A boy of about seven was crouching by her, with a cup of water and hunk of bread in his hands. He had enormous brown eyes, which were fixed on her face.

"What's your name?" he asked in the same island dialect that whoever had spoken to her on the first night had used.

"Cass," she replied. "And yours?"

"Lion," he replied with a roar.

Cass smiled despite herself and touching his blond curly hair gently said, "The name suits you. We have the same hair."

The boy nodded seriously.

"Yes, but you have skin like goat's milk," he replied. "While mine is like sweet cacao."

"You are much luckier than me," Cass agreed.

"I will call you Goatsmilk," he announced. "Now eat this please, Goatsmilk. It will make you stronger." And after handing her the bread and cup of water, he wandered off.

For the first few days, Cass spent most of her time lying on her mattress either crying or dozing, her feelings rotating from fury with Bang and Leila, and Bastien and Enzo, to recurring terror of her encounter with Varen. However, she did manage to come out of her own head enough to look around at Bang's other slaves. They were all women and children, ranging in age from two years to about thirty, and were mostly Far Islanders. Cass was no expert but they looked malnourished to her and, with the exception of Lion, they had a listlessness that suggested a lack of hope as well as food. Coming from Minaris, where slaving had been outlawed for many years, Cass's sense of justice was outraged that such a practice was allowed.

On her third evening, when the others went up on deck at sundown, Cass decided she should go too, if only to show Bang that she was not entirely defeated. She had begun making plans to escape from the boat at the first opportunity she got. And if that didn't work, she would somehow get word to Elsba – she remembered her address in Villuvia. *Surely Elsba would help her?* Cass thought, and allowed herself to daydream about Elsba and her cohorts from the Company – bold, fearless, sword-wielding women coming to rescue her and the other slaves.

Walking up the stairs was painful but she made it up on deck. The wind had dropped and the air hung like a sultry fog. Storm clouds, like vast towers of candyfloss, were banked up on the horizon. She took her meagre bowl of rice with a tiny bit of salted fish, and went and sat with Lion.

"So who sold you, Goatsmilk?" he asked.

"A girl called Leila. She tricked me into her house and then drugged me," Cass replied.

"But why were you not with your parents?" Lion looked puzzled.

"My parents are dead, and I was – am – on my way to a place called the Island of Women." Lion still looked confused but Cass didn't have the heart to continue so she just said, "It's a long story, I'll tell you another time. Who sold you?"

Lion's face darkened.

"My father sold me after the pirates came and robbed our village. We had nothing and he said he had to. He cried like a baby." Here Lion did a sour imitation of wailing. "He said it was for my own good, but he did it for the gold. When I am big, I will buy the sharpest sword in the whole world and return home and I will kill him like this." And he lunged forward with his hand, as if he were holding a knife, his eyes narrowed to determined slits.

"Does no one ever try to escape from here?" Cass asked.

Lion looked at her as if she were mad.

"Where are you going to escape to? The sea is full of sharks that would eat you long before you got anywhere near the shore. Slavery is bad but it is better than death."

Is it? Cass wondered. She pointed at a distant island that was looming out of the sea.

"Do you see that island? Do you have any idea what it is?"

"Yes, the sailors were talking about it but I can't remember its name. Samos, Sames…"

"Samay?" Cass asked, the name coming back to her from maps on the Palace Ship. Her time there already seemed like a dream, when in reality barely a week had elapsed since the Palace Ship had sailed into Tarn.

"Yes, that's right. Samay," Lion confirmed.

The island, Cass remembered, lay about a hundred miles to the south-west of Tarn and was only about fifty miles from the Island of Women. The Island of Women now hovered in Cass's mind like a kind of heaven.

"Anyway, the sailors say we will stop there tomorrow and maybe pick up some more slaves. But the real reason is so they can drink." And

Lion did another gesture of draining a glass and then transformed his face to a woozy drunk, gently hiccupping.

Cass's heart leaped. Maybe she would be able to escape! Her thoughts were clearly written all over her face, because Lion said, "And we will be chained up in the hold."

The boat pulled into the harbour at Samay in the late afternoon the following day and, leaving just a couple of sailors on board, Bang and the others made their way to the Inn of the Black Octopus. As Lion had predicted, all the slaves including Cass were chained up in the hold. Despite the almost suffocating heat, Cass spent hours desperately trying to open the locks of her chains with a toothpick she had found on deck but it was no use, they wouldn't move.

"Give up, Goatsmilk," Lion said sleepily. "Let us try to stand next to each other at the slave market and then perhaps the same person will buy us."

Cass smiled at him but at that moment the toothpick splintered and broke. She threw it away in exasperation.

"I cannot give up," she replied. "Even when we

are working together in an emerald mine in the Far Isles or wherever we end up, I will not give up. You will see."

It was a couple of nights later that Cass and the other slaves were woken by shouting and an almighty crash from the side of the boat. It sounded like another boat had rammed into them. They all sat up, instantly awake, watching the door, listening to the sound of footsteps ringing down the stairs. It was not Bang who appeared, but one of the sailors.

"Come now," he said to Cass. Cass was more intrigued than frightened – was someone here to rescue her? Had Rip come? Had Elsba, somehow heard…

There was just a sliver of moon that night with few stars, and it was dark on the deck with only a couple of lanterns lit. One was immediately shoved in Cass's face.

"That's the girl," a male voice said, but Cass could only see the silhouettes of the men. What was going on? She could feel the tension crackling through the air like a thunderstorm.

"Very well," Cass heard Bang say with a sigh. "And my sincere apologies to your master. I had no idea."

Who could his master be? Cass wondered.

"Oh really, fat man?" the male voice said in a Far Isles accent. "Not according to the landlady in Samay. She said you swore that you had no such girl on board. I think you didn't want to lose the gold that you would make out of her in Riza."

"I promise you it was not deliberate," Bang said, his voice ingratiating. "I genuinely believed it was not the same girl. If there is anything I can offer you by way of compensation for your trouble, I would gladly oblige. I am carrying a cargo of summer wine from the Mid Isles. You are welcome to that."

"How very kind of you! You'd better hand over your silvers too, fat man," the voice said.

The lantern light fell on the man speaking and Cass looked at the young Far Islander. He was as broad as a bull, with a shaved head and a sword by his side. In a moment of terrible realization she suddenly knew who his master was just as he said, "Cassandra, let me introduce myself. I am Kov. My master, Varen, is going to be thrilled to see you."

Black spots danced in front of Cass's eyes and the bones in her body seemed to melt away. She would have crumpled in a heap on the deck had the sailor not held her up. The pirate saw this and laughed. "Right, let's get you aboard our boat," he said.

Cass was filled with the same terror she had felt with Varen and it made time move very slowly. The sailor passed her over to one of the pirates, who took her roughly by the arm.

The pirate ship was alongside the slave boat, roped to it, and the pirate took her to the far end to cross. He muttered some disgusting things to her and called to the others left on board the boat. A feeling of such horror and revulsion rose up in Cass that it swallowed her fear and she knew as clearly as she knew her name that she mustn't get on board that boat. What had Lion said to her? That being a slave was better than death. Well, being a prisoner of the pirates wasn't. She would definitely rather die, even if it meant being eaten by sharks.

So when the pirate tried to pass Cass across to the other ship, she turned and kicked him as hard as she could in the face, which gave her just a moment, a fraction of a second. She launched herself off the boat, flinging her body as far out into the sea as she could, and falling deep down into the inky water.

Furious shouts cut through the air as the pirates scrambled into a rowing boat and before Cass could swim any distance, they were on the water, following.

"Give yourself up!" she heard Kov bellow. "I always catch my prey, Cassandra, and when I do it will be the worse for you!"

The sea was calm and Cass swam with all her might towards land. But a strong current held her back, and the rowing boat surged closer.

This is hopeless, she thought despairingly. The rowing boat was barely six metres away. *They will reach me in a few minutes and if they don't a shark will soon get me. But I would rather drown than be caught*, she decided and, expelling all the breath from her body, she let herself slip under the water.

"No, you wouldn't," a voice said, appearing in her head with no warning, clear as a bell. "But stay underwater as much as you can and let the current take you. Let the current take you," the voice repeated. It was Lin, Cass realized with a jolt.

"Where are you?" Cass asked.

"I am at home, Cass, but I am with you too," she replied.

"How can you do that?" Cass asked her. "Am I no longer obtuse?"

"You most certainly are and it is incredibly difficult, even with the ring. I may not be able to stay with you for long," Lin said. "So you must listen carefully."

Cass did as Lin told her, and she was drawn into the very centre of the current, which was swift and strong. It propelled her quickly away from the pirates.

"Good," Lin's voice said.

"But it's taking me out to sea," Cass protested.

"I know. You need to get away from the pirates first."

"But what about sharks?"

"There are none around for the moment. Now

try to relax, Cass, you will need all your energy later, trust me."

Cass glanced back at the two ships and the pirates' rowing boat. She could see them desperately shining lanterns on the water, looking for her. She was too far away from them now for any beam of light to reach her, she realized with relief, but still close enough that if they rowed in the right direction they could quickly get to her.

On and on the current swept her along, like a river surging through the waters of the Straits. Soon the slave boat was only a dot in the distance and, except for Lin in her head, she was entirely alone in the middle of the huge deep dark sea.

In time the current weakened and brought her a little further towards the land, but she was still a good mile out.

"You need to swim now, swim fast, Cass. There are sharks approaching," Lin said, as calmly as she could. Cass screamed with terror, and swam as swiftly as she could. She drew nearer to the shore but her limbs were so heavy with cold and exhaustion that her pace slackened.

"Try, Cass, you must try," Lin urged. "The sharks have gone away again but they may be back. Please, Cass, swim just a bit further and the waves will carry you to the shore."

Cass swam on as far as she could but eventually, as the dawn was breaking, exhaustion got the better of her. She lost consciousness and gently sank under the water.

Cass found herself lying on the sofa in Mrs Potts's sitting room in Minaris, looking out over the Square of Seas. It was winter and the room was warm with a crackling fire in the grate. Cass felt exhausted but cosy and happy. Someone had left a cup of tea and a cloud cake on the table in front of her and she was just reaching for them when the door opened and Lin came in.

"That's such a coincidence! You were just talking to me in my dreams," Cass said. "At least I think it was a dream…" she faltered.

"Cass, you need to come with me now," Lin said, taking her by the hands, and trying to pull her off the sofa.

"No, Lin, not now. I'm too tired," Cass protested.

"Cass," Lin replied, her face deadly serious. "It's very important that you come."

"Here, let me drink this tea at least," Cass said, reaching for the cup.

"No, there is no time," Lin insisted as she pulled Cass up and led her out of the door and down the stairs to the basement.

"Why are we coming down here?" Cass asked. *Perhaps it is something to do with Tig,* she thought, craning her neck looking for her. Lin didn't answer. She opened the door to a cupboard. But instead of the normal mess of mops and brooms there was another staircase that Lin led her down.

"I've never seen this before," Cass said, amazed, as they went down and down. She heard the sound of waves. "I never knew the sea was beneath our house."

"You live on the Square of Seas, Cass, so of course the sea is beneath you," Lin replied. "Come on, you need to hurry," she said, practically pulling

166

her down the last flight.

Cass found herself standing with Lin in the surf, on a beach with white sand and palm trees. It was hot but there was a strong breeze and the skies were full of seabirds calling to one another. Cass looked back to where the house and the staircase had been but they had disappeared.

"I'm so confused," Cass said and she would have been frightened if it hadn't been so strange. "Am I asleep?" she asked, and then suddenly another much darker thought occurred to her. "Am I dead?"

"You are somewhere in between," Lin replied, pointing a little way down the beach to a dark shape huddled on the sand. "And Cass, you need to go back right now, or it will be too late."

The memories of all that had happened hit Cass like a wave, smack in the face.

"No," she said. "No, I don't want to go back. The pirates will only find me again and kill me. I'd rather die now."

"You need to be brave," Lin said, taking her in her arms. "I know things have been difficult for you, but life is sometimes. And there is so much more to come, some amazing things. If you leave your life now, you will never know any of that. If you can just wake up, it will be all right. But you have to go now, or it will be too late."

"No," Cass said with a groan. "I just want to go back to the sofa in the sitting room."

"You must go, Cass, please – for us," a voice said. And Cass looked round to see a man and woman standing by her. They put their arms round her too. Tears streamed down her face.

"Why did you leave me?" she cried.

"We have never left you, we are always with you," her mother said.

"And we had no choice about the end of our lives," her father said. "But you do have a choice, Cass. Look, people are coming who will help you."

Cass watched as two women went over to her body. One of them started pumping her chest.

"Cass, you must leave now," her father said to her sternly.

"If you will only go and try, Cass, you will get the opportunity to do good things," her mother urged.

Cass looked at her mother. "You promise?"

"It won't be easy, but yes I promise. Now go!" she said.

"Very well," Cass replied wearily. She gasped as the ground fell from beneath her with a whoosh, as if she were falling through the sky. The next thing she knew she was on her side and vomiting sour salty seawater. Every part of her hurt and it took all her effort just to open her eyes. She looked down the beach but Lin and her parents had gone. The women were bending over her, smiling.

"We thought we'd lost you," one of them said.

"Where am I?" Cass managed to ask.

"Why child, this is the Island of Women," she replied.

THE
LONGEST WORLD

The Island of Women

Tali

Samay

SOUTHERN ARCH

THE AVE

KATIRAN ARCH

The Island of Women, the Mid Isles
Midday

XI

Nightly Ramblings

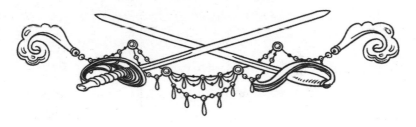

Between them, the fisherwomen carried Cass to the infirmary.

Cass remembered little of what happened next – just vague memories of being examined by gentle but practical hands and wrapped in clean-smelling blankets, before drinking bitter night draughts. And then a deadened nothingness, cruelly followed by terrible nightmares that flung Cass back into reality, sweating and screaming. And then there was further kindness and further bitter draughts. At some point a low voice asked her name, and she managed to murmur *Cassandra Malvino* but more from habit than conviction.

Because really, she wasn't entirely sure who she was.

It was the bright sunlight that woke her on the third day. She opened her eyes to see a woman in a long pale blue dress looking out of the window by her bed. She would have screamed had the woman not looked so kind and calm. *The Island of Women*, her brain managed to think, *that is where I am.*

"The sun," the woman announced, her face smiling broadly. "It's been raining for seven days solidly and I was beginning to feel like we would never see the sun again. Now, how are you feeling?"

A surge of panic shot through Cass as she remembered the pirates and the slave ship. She sat bolt upright and demanded, "Have they come for me? The pirates? Have they been here?" she asked desperately.

"No, no, Cass, there are no pirates here and there never will be," the woman reassured her. "You are quite safe. I give you my word. Now, I'd like you to try and breathe and relax, then I want to take your pulse."

And without waiting for Cass to answer, she came over to the bed, and after they sat in silence for a few minutes while Cass tried to relax, she took her pulse.

"I'm Meg by the way," the woman said, and then stared into space as she counted the beats of Cass's heart. Cass felt like her whole body, and particularly her brain, had been through a washing mangle.

"A little fast still," Meg pronounced after a minute. "And how's your stomach after the seawater?"

Cass could barely remember where her stomach was but she knew she had to make some reply.

"I think it feels all right," she said.

"Good. Now how about I bring you some breakfast? Or lunch, I suppose, and then I know that Lady Sigh is eager to see you, so do you feel up to walking to her house later? It's just across there." She gestured vaguely out of the window.

Cass felt another rush of panic rise up in her at the thought of leaving her narrow bed with its comfortingly starched sheets, and to her surprise and embarrassment, her face crinkled up and hot tears began to pour from her eyes.

"Oh, my dear," Meg cried. "There is no hurry for any of that. Lady Sigh can wait!" she joked.

"Here is a handkerchief. Now dry your tears while I fetch you some food." And she bustled off, promising to be back as soon as she could.

Cass must have fallen back to sleep because she woke to find Meg returning, carrying a bowl of something.

"I'm sorry that took such a long time. We don't have much call for soup in this climate. But it's just the thing for you." And she put the bowl down on the table beside the bed as she helped Cass to sit up. She then fed her spoonfuls of the soup as if Cass were a baby. It tasted delicious, spicy and creamy, but Cass only managed half a bowl full before she fell back on her pillows, exhausted with the effort.

"Well done," Meg said. "Now since the sun is still shining and it's a beautiful afternoon, why don't I put a chair by this window? You can sit and look out and see what is going on. And then if you feel too tired you can just get back into bed and sleep a bit more."

Cass still felt reluctant to leave her bed but she nodded in agreement to please Meg, and slowly got up. Her legs felt weak and strange but they carried her the couple of steps to the chair. And she managed to sit there for ten minutes or so, looking out but seeing nothing, before the desire to get back into bed became too much for her.

And that was how Cass passed the next few days. She moved from bed to chair, chair to bed, each day being coaxed by the kindly Meg to eat and to spend longer in the chair, to try and take some interest in the view, to notice the bustle of the world outside. Slowly little battles were won – Cass managed to have a bath and wash her hair. She ate a whole meal. Some clothes were found for her and she got dressed. She went for a couple of walks with Meg by her side. And gradually the daytime tears stopped flowing as much, and the terror and screaming lessened at night as the monsters – the faces of Kov and the pirates, but also of Lion and the other slaves she had left behind – receded back into their lair.

It was one evening after Cass had been on the Island for about a week that Lady Sigh came to see her. Cass heard Meg talking in a low voice to someone and then a few moments later, a slight, blond woman appeared. She was as fair as Cass, and so otherworldly, dressed as she was in a pale grey silk dress cut formally in the Minarian fashion, that Cass thought she looked like she had stepped out of one of the old paintings that lined Madame Carpera's walls.

"Cass," she said, taking her hand as if they were old friends. She had a low gruff voice that was at odds with her looks. "I am so pleased to meet you. I knew your mother of course, and then Rip wrote to me…"

"Rip?" Cass could not help herself interrupting. "He wrote to you? When?"

Lady Sigh smiled slightly. "He wrote to me after you left the Palace Ship in Tarn. He was concerned about you – he said you had disappeared. Do you feel up to telling me what happened?"

Cass nodded and told Lady Sigh about being sold to Bang by Leila, and then the pirates coming for her. She did not give Lady Sigh any explanation of why the pirates were looking for her, but Lady Sigh did not query this, to Cass's relief.

Perhaps she knows, Cass thought, as Lady Sigh

said instead, "What a time you have had. But luck was certainly with you that last night – to be washed twenty miles down the Avenian Straits and survive is a miracle."

Cass nodded but she felt shy of telling Lady Sigh about Lin helping her, knowing that magic was outlawed on the Island. Instead she swallowed nervously and confessed, "I am so afraid that the pirates will have harmed the slaves on the ship I was on. I was particular friends with a young boy called Lion, and I feel so guilty about leaving him. Also," Cass admitted. "I am worried that the pirates will come here, looking for me."

"Well, I haven't heard any reports of the pirates harming slaves, and it doesn't sound as if you had any choice other than to leave your young friend," Lady Sigh said kindly. "And you must not worry about the pirates coming here. Firstly, they will not think that you are alive – that bit of sea is notorious for its terrible currents and for sharks. But if they decided by some miracle that you survived, they will look on the neighbouring islands, not as far south as here. And even if they do come, they will not arrive unseen and there are a hundred hiding places up in the mountains and deep in the jungle that I know about that they do not. So really you must not worry. We will keep you safe, I promise. Does that help?" she asked giving Cass's hand a squeeze.

Cass nodded again in reply.

"Your mother was an amazing woman," Lady Sigh went on. "So kind-hearted and talented. You know, you're a great deal like her."

The thought of being compared with her mother sent tears to Cass's eyes. Seeing her in her dreams when she was drowning had been both upsetting and comforting for her.

"I am not kind-hearted or talented," she replied, thinking shamefully of her thieving.

"That is not what I have heard from Rip. He said you are an amazing acrobat," Lady Sigh said. She went on carefully, "Everyone makes mistakes, Cass, and to move forward you must forgive yourself."

Rip told her about the thieving, Cass thought with a wince of shame.

"If you don't," Lady Sigh continued, "you will be stuck like this and then your life will be wasted.

And, moreover, the pirates will have won. You are young and you are strong, and you can still do many incredible things." Lady Sigh squeezed her hands and let them go, rising to her feet. "Now I must go back to my rooms and let you get some sleep." She turned to go but then stopped. "I'm sorry, I was almost forgetting that I have these for you." And she handed her several envelopes addressed in Mrs Potts's looping handwriting.

Cass was too tired to read the letters that night, and then put them to one side for a couple of days, as she couldn't face Mrs Potts's rant about her selfishness at running away that Cass imagined they would contain. But when she finally did work up the courage to open them they were not quite as she expected.

Time and distance had worked a little magic, and Mrs Potts wrote to Cass that although she had been very angry and upset at first, she had had "a long hard think". She could see she "hadn't been all she could have in the way of a mother" to Cass, and that she should have allowed Cass to do what she wished with her life. This apology touched Cass deeply. And while so much had happened to Cass in the two and a half months since she had left, she gathered that nothing much had happened there at all, which Cass found curiously comforting.

Most of Mrs Potts's letters seemed taken up with admonitions to Cass that she hoped she was looking after her skin, keeping her fingernails clean and combing her hair, as well as talk of the weather, which was either unseasonably hot or cold, and her new lodger, a fortune teller who was "a terribly gifted young man with beautiful manners". The greatest event seemed to be that one of the neighbours' cats had had kittens in the kitchen, and even more selfishly on Tig's day off, so there had been "quite simply chaos". She ended each letter in the same way:

So my dearest Cassandra, Tig and I send you our love across the sea. We hope that we will see you before not too long so I will only say, goodbye for now. Your loving guardian,
Emmelina Potts

Before she arrived, Cass had imagined the Island of Women as a colony of about fifty or so eccentric women living in a collection of untidy huts in the middle of the jungle. But, as she found out, she could not have been more wrong.

For a start, most of the valley where the village – for that was the best description of what it was – lay had been cleared of jungle to grow crops and graze animals. The village itself consisted of an orderly series of old stone buildings, interspersed with courtyards full of fruit trees, and linked by covered walkways that gave some protection against the fierce heat or the torrential rain that seemed to be the two types of weather and seasons that the Island enjoyed.

"The heat is not so bad now but wait and see in a few months," Meg said with a laugh. "You'll feel like a loaf of bread being baked in an oven."

As they walked, Meg told Cass a little about the long history of the Island, which was founded more than five hundred years before under the rule of the Tysian Dynasty, and its motto, which roughly translated from ancient Tysian, was basically that no woman or child could ever be refused sanctuary on the Island. Meg pointed out the nursery, the schoolrooms, the kitchen, with its huge vegetable gardens, and the dining room, the different dormitory blocks, the library, the baths, the seamstress, the laundry, and right in the middle of it all was Lady Sigh's circular house.

There were at least four hundred women on the Island, and not just from the Mid Isles; there were a good smattering of Far Islanders, Far Southerners and Northerners such as herself and Lady Sigh. Much of the work and life of the Island was focused on the orphan children who were brought from all over the Mid Isles to be cared for. The boys stayed until they were seven, and then homes were found for them on nearby islands while the girls, Meg explained, usually stayed until they were about sixteen, when most left to make their way in the world. But some, like herself, remained. All the girls were taught how to read and write, in mathematics and science, and were also trained in a skill so they could find useful work – many became apothecaries, nurses and teachers, Meg said, but also carpenters, boat builders, notaries and scholars, players or musicians.

There were other things that Cass hadn't expected too; for a start there were men there.

Plenty, particularly in the tiny harbour that lay at one end of the Island.

"Men are allowed to come here," Meg explained with a laugh. "They just can't live here."

And the Island was *so* beautiful; neither Lin or Rip's comments, nor her mother's picture, had prepared Cass for the smoky-purple mountains, the lush, luminescent greenness of the jungle, bisected by joyfully bright flowering vines, or the butterflies the size of her palm and the clouds of pink parakeets.

On one of their walks, Meg steered her towards a door, with a sign above it that read *Garment Store,* saying that they must sort out Cass's clothes. Meg explained to the lady who ran it that Cass had arrived with nothing, and would need normal clothes and something to wear for acrobatics.

"Come and choose what you want," the lady said, taking her to a section of shelves, crammed full of neatly folded clothes. "What do you normally wear? Dresses, or breeches?"

As a Minarian, Cass had only ever worn dresses, except for acrobatics. She decided that it was time for a change.

"Breeches please," she replied. The lady appraised her and selected three pairs, which she held up to Cass for inspection.

"They look broadly the right size but I'll give you a belt too. And let's find you some shirts." She ran her finger over the piles as she pulled out some options. Cass chose the more boyish cotton ones, in plain white or stripes.

"Good choices," the lady said. "Now how about a couple of waistcoats, a jacket and a shawl as it can get cold at night for a few months of the year. And do you want to help yourself to underclothes and nightwear. I will give you a needle and thread to sew your name into the clothes so they don't get lost at the laundry. Oh, and towels – I will give you two as you need to take your own to the bathhouse. And I happen to have a spare comb here which might be useful," she added, eyeing Cass's mane.

On the way back to the infirmary, Meg said to Cass, "Lady Sigh wondered if you would help out in the schoolroom tomorrow for a few hours. They are very short-staffed and it would be such a help." Cass felt a twinge of panic but she nodded as bravely as she could.

"It will be fine," Meg reassured her. "And I think you will like Annabella, who runs the schoolroom."

Annabella was only a few years older than Cass. She was very slight, with ink-stained fingers, large intelligent brown eyes and messy, floppy brown hair that was always escaping from its pins, however fiercely she clipped it back. She immediately set Cass to work teaching a large table of mischievous six-year-olds how to read and write the letters T, V and E. In fact, most of Cass's morning seemed to be spent keeping order, sorting out their quarrels and drying tears. But then, when the children ran off to have lunch, Cass collected their books and felt a sense of pride and amazement by the neat rows of letters they had written.

"Well done," Annabella said, looking over her shoulder. "So where are you from, Cass?"

When Cass replied, "Minaris," Annabella's face lit up.

"How amazing! My dream is to visit there, particularly the Great Library, and talk to the scholars and the naturalists. Dr Abraim is my absolute hero – I have all his books. Are you interested in such things?"

Cass was about to reply no, not really, but there was something about Annabella that made Cass want to please her, so instead she said, "Yes, a little, although I don't know much about them."

"Oh, you must come and see my collection then." And she led her to the back of the schoolroom where there was a lean-to shack stuffed full of what Tig would have called, with a horrified expression, "creepy crawlies". But Annabella proudly showed Cass her ants' and bees' nests that were split open at the side with panes of glass.

"Look, these are Fortuna ants, which you only find in this part of the Mid Isles. See the distinctive white stripe that runs down the centre of their backs. There's the Queen with her swollen abdomen, and the other ants swarming around her. And look, here are my Peace bees, again native to the Mid Isles. They are called that because they have no sting – otherwise I might not have been so brave in taking the nest from a tree."

Annabella started to tell Cass about their life

cycles and Cass began to ask her more questions.

"And you must meet my beetles," said Annabella, pulling her over to a large glass case full of old bits of wood, swarming with multi-coloured beetles. "Oh, and this is Nog and Tog, my giant Fishbone spiders. Don't you think they are rather wonderful?" Cass's new-found enthusiasm did not extend to Nog and Tog and she tried not to flinch at the huge hairy beasts, focusing instead on a large bowl of old fruit that was covered in feasting Vendoven butterflies.

"Ah, there you are," a voice said and Cass turned round to see Meg.

"Oh, I'm sorry," Cass replied.

"Don't apologize," said Meg. "You look like you've had a good morning?"

Cass nodded and thanked Annabella, who raised her eyebrows, saying, "It was you who helped me, not the other way round. Can you come again tomorrow?"

"Yes, I would like that," Cass replied truthfully. And she felt a lessening inside her, as if a heavy weight, placed deep in her stomach by Enzo, Varen and the others, had been slightly lifted.

THE
LONGEST WORLD

The Island of Women

Tali

SOUTHERN ARCH

Samay

THE AVE

KATIRAN ARCH

The Island of Women

The Island of Women, the Mid Isles
Late afternoon

XII

Turtle Hatching

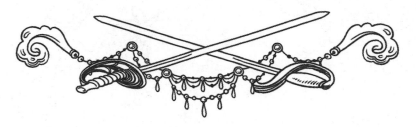

A few days later, Cass received a note with her name written in very neat, spiky handwriting. It was from Pela, the woman who taught fighting and acrobatics. The note asked for Cass to go and see her that evening before supper. She taught at the pavilion near the beach – Cass just had to follow the path by the laundry and she would come to it.

Later, dressed in her breeches and a camisole, and feeling nervous, Cass walked past the laundry. White sand began to wash over the stone path and Cass could clearly hear the swish-swash of the waves not far away. To her left, she saw a wooden pavilion and she made her way over to it.

A slender woman with long dark brown hair stood in the middle of the pavilion like a conductor, as she directed a gaggle of children clearing up mats into neat piles. When they were done, she clapped her hands and they lined up in a neat row, bowed to her, and then politely filed out. Cass smiled as they pushed past her and started giggling, returning to their normal boisterous selves.

From a distance Pela looked young, but once Cass came closer she could see that her face was lined, her olive skin marked with freckles and sunspots, and her long hair was streaked with grey.

"Ah, you must be Cass," she said. "How nice it is to meet you at last. I've been told that Malvino was your father, and you are keen to audition for the Circus Boat in Minaris next year. Do you have an acrobatic routine?"

"Yes," Cass replied and, feeling increasingly nervous under Pela's exacting gaze, she took herself through her old routine of stretches and warm-ups. She couldn't believe how stiff she was. But once she started doing the floor routine, her body obeyed her and she relaxed a little, executing all the manoeuvres adequately if not exceptionally. And it felt good to move her body again. Pela watched her closely, passing no comment until she had finished.

"You are a good acrobat, Cass, and you could be a really excellent one. But you will need to work very hard. Are you prepared to do that?"

"Yes," Cass replied. "Being an acrobat is what I have always dreamed of."

"Good," said Pela. "Then we will make it happen. Now, is there anything else you want to ask me before the others arrive?"

Cass had been thinking a good deal about Elsba and Idaliz, and found herself blurting out, "Would you teach me to fight? I met a woman named Elsba who learned with you."

Pela looked surprised. "Where did you meet her?" she asked carefully.

"I met her onboard the merchant's boat that I left Minaris on."

"Oh, I see," said Pela. "And what sort of fighting? Do you just mean hand-to-hand combat, which most girls here learn, or sword fighting, too?"

"Both please," Cass replied.

"Very well." Pela nodded. "I will be interested to see how you get on."

"Thank you so much!" Cass said, delighted.

A gaggle of about ten teenage girls had appeared and were hovering at the edge of the pavilion.

"Come in, everyone. This is Cass and she will be doing acrobatic training with you. Cass, all these girls do acrobatics for fun, although we take it very seriously."

"Some of the girls swim every morning," Pela went on. "And I want you to do the same, to build up your strength."

Cass gave a start. The sea had become the stuff of nightmares for her, and she couldn't imagine even paddling in it again, let alone swimming.

As if Pela could read her mind, she said, "You need to face your fears, Cass. The first few times will be hard but I guarantee that within a couple of weeks the sea will hold no terror for you."

Everyone on the Island worked hard, and Lady

Sigh ensured that Cass was left with no time to brood. She woke at dawn and swam a mile before breakfast with the other girls. Her mornings were spent helping Annabella with teaching, and after lunch and the short siesta that everyone took to avoid the hottest part of the day, she worked in the kitchens, preparing the evening meal. She then did laundry before she trained with Pela in either acrobatics or fighting. Then, so exhausted that she could hardly speak, Cass would stagger into supper, after which she either helped Meg in the infirmary or studied the books that Annabella gave her, before falling fast asleep soon after the dark night descended.

Each day Cass inched a little further back to her old self, or it is perhaps more accurate to say a version of her old self, because she was never entirely as she was before. Her nightmares receded enough for her to leave the infirmary, and she moved into Annabella's room, which she liked, despite Annabella's ever-increasing collection of stray animals that also lived there.

Cass grew to love them all but her favourite was Von, a large tortoiseshell cat. Annabella had found him when he was just a kitten on the neighbouring Island of Villuvia. He had been viciously attacked and his wounds were infected, and the poor creature was barely alive. But Annabella had brought him back to the Island, and together with the apothecary, she had nursed him back to health.

Much to their delight, he had survived and thrived. He could be found wandering all around the village during the day but at night he stayed in Annabella's room. He took to curling up on Cass's bed with her and when she woke, haunted by her dreams or panicking over Lion's fate, it was his purring presence that comforted her.

One afternoon, Lady Sigh arranged for several of the older women to gather together in her rooms, and they spent a happy hour with Cass, telling her everything they remembered about her mother. Cass had spent most of her life since the fire avoiding thinking about her mother and father, because she thought she would find it too painful.

But seeing them so vividly while she was drowning had somehow allowed her to think about their deaths properly. And although she still missed them, she found to her relief that the wound had largely healed and she could examine it without flinching. And so the women's tales of a clever, brave young woman, with a strong mischievous streak, made her happy, not sad.

"And you didn't mind that she was magical? And went off to practise fortune telling in Minaris?" Cass asked Lady Sigh.

"No, not in the least," Lady Sigh replied, and then laughed. "In fact, after she had hypnotised most of the animals on the Island, making the cocks crow at lunchtime and the cook's dog walk backwards, we all agreed that she needed to leave!" And then she went on more seriously, "Your mother was very talented, Cass, but I knew that she would use that talent wisely so I was only pleased for her."

Lady Sigh also showed Cass her mother's entry in the leaving book; a pen and ink drawing of an orange tree and a butterfly. Written along a branch were the words, *May some part of me return here one day*, and it was initialled AD for Amelia Durrante, which had been her name before she married.

"And your mother's wish has come true, Cass," Lady Sigh pointed out. "For some part of her has returned here with you."

It was after Cass had been on the Island for a little over a month that Lady Sigh unexpectedly summoned her to her study one afternoon. Cass was in the middle of a sword-fighting lesson but she hurried over to the circular house, and climbed the stairs to Lady Sigh's study on the first floor, knocking on the door.

The room was smoky from the incense Lady Sigh burned to ward off insects. She was sitting at her desk, bent over paperwork, but she immediately got to her feet when Cass walked in. She took Cass's hand and led her to the sofa. Her face was so pale and concerned that Cass braced herself for bad news.

"Cass, I have just received a terrible message concerning Bastien. Apparently he had some kind of seizure following an argument with Varen the pirate chief, and has died."

Cass gasped. "Died?" she repeated.

Lady Sigh nodded. "I'm afraid so."

"I wonder why they were arguing?" said Cass, still in a state of shock.

"It appears they had struck up a friendship of sorts and were together when they ran into the Minarian Navy. A fight ensued, which Varen won, but he believed for some reason that Bastien had led them into an ambush. The two men argued fiercely, causing Bastien to collapse. He died almost immediately and then Varen took charge of the Palace Ship."

"But what of Rip and Enzo? And Ornella?"

"Ornella was released and is en route to Minaris." Cass thought of Narina, Cass's cousin, before Lady Sigh said, "Unfortunately Rip and Enzo were not so lucky."

Cass held her breath in horror. *Not Rip, please let nothing have happened to Rip*, she prayed.

"Varen took the boys on to his own boat as prisoners, setting sail immediately for the Far Isles," Lady Sigh continued and as she watched

Cass's face turn even paler and her eyes widen with distress, she said as reassuringly as she could, "He has no reason to harm them and King Lycus has, of course, immediately dispatched as many ships as he could spare to try to find them."

"And what of the Palace Ship?" said Cass, thinking of the sailors on board that she knew.

"That is the strangest part of the tale. I am told that Varen instructed his men to tow the ship into the bay at Tarn. Then the crew was forced to swim to the shore while the ship was left as his gift, Varen said, to the people of Tarn from their new King. They did as he bid them, arriving late at night. By dawn there was apparently nothing left of the mighty Palace Ship but a few planks floating in the water."

That evening, Cass lay on her bed with Von on her stomach, trying to come to terms with what Lady Sigh had told her. She had spent a lot of time hating Bastien and Enzo for dragging her into their plans, but that hate dissolved into sadness over

Bastien's death and pity for Enzo being captured by the pirates. For Rip she felt acutely concerned.

Over the previous weeks she had found her thoughts wandering ever increasingly to Rip, and missing him in a way that she didn't really understand. He had been so kind, and had risked his life to help her, despite hardly knowing her.

Cass must have fallen asleep because she woke later in the evening to find Annabella quietly moving around the room, gathering various objects – some pencils, a long ruler, a notebook.

"What are you doing?" Cass asked.

"Oh, I'm sorry I woke you. I think the baby turtles will be hatching on the beach. Won't you come and see them?"

Cass knew that Annabella was making a particular study of the turtles that year, and in the month or two before Cass had arrived, had spent many nights watching and recording the great beasts lumbering out of the water and l aying their eggs in nests in the sand. The baby turtles would then hatch, she had explained to Cass, and leave their nests at night when there were fewer predators around, and make their way down to the sea.

Cass felt wide awake and in need of distraction so she allowed Annabella's enthusiasm to lead her down to the beach.

Their way was lit by a large silver moon that hung like a giant disc in the navy, star-scattered sky. Cass was slightly sceptical as to whether they would see anything but sure enough, as soon as they walked a little way along the beach, they could see hordes of tiny turtles appearing out of hollows in the sand as if by magic and then making their way down to the sea. Her scepticism melted away, and Cass spent an hour or so helping Annabella with her recording and sketching of the creatures attempting the first journey of their lives.

They walked back, splashing through the waves as they broke on the shore. Little flashes of white light sparked off their feet.

"Did you know," Cass said to Annabella, "that those sparks are given off by tiny creatures too small for us to see."

"No! Is that true?" Annabella replied excitedly. "That is amazing. I wonder whether they are visible with magnification. Who told you such a thing?"

"Just a friend," Cass replied sadly, wondering where in the Longest World Rip was now.

THE
LONGEST WORLD

THE FAR ISLES

Tali

The Island of Women

SOUTHERN

Parma

Samay

THE A

The Island of Women

Tali

THE AW

TIRAN ARCHIPELAGO

The Island of Women and
the Island of Tali, the Mid Isles
Ten o'clock at night

XIII

An Unexpected Visitor

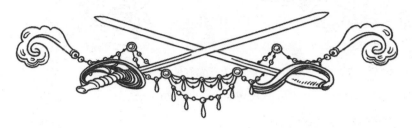

The weeks flew past, turning into months. The constant heat and Cass's busyness combined to give her little sense of time passing but had she been in Minaris, summer and autumn would have been and gone and the winter would have arrived bringing the seasonal flood and freeze, as the year came to its end. In fact, it was Lady Sigh mentioning to her that they must arrange her passage back to Minaris very soon for the Circus auditions in the early spring that made her realize that she had been on the Island over half a year.

All Cass really noticed was that she had got a

great deal better at acrobatics and fighting and her dreams of the future were still firmly focused on her next audition with Ravellous. The daily swims and practising meant that she had become lean and strong, and she felt as if someone had inserted an iron rod in her shoulders, making her stand up straight at all times.

Was she happy? she sometimes wondered and decided if happiness was a sense of peaceful exhaustion, of slowly working towards a goal, then she had achieved it. In many ways it seemed to her that she had always lived on the Island, and that her old life had been a dream – it was only when she wrote and received letters from Mrs Potts, Lin and Tig that she thought of Minaris at all. And yet sometimes, especially in the golden light of the late afternoon, she found herself yearning for something she couldn't quite identify.

Beyond the quiet shores of the Island of Women, the Mid and Far Isles had descended into a state of turmoil. Varen himself might have gone to the Far Isles but he had left plenty of his men in the Mid Isles, and the pirates' ever-increasing power meant that trading had all but ceased and food shortages were a serious problem. Although the search for Enzo and Rip went on, most of the Navy's energies were focused on escorting flotillas of merchants' ships providing essential supplies to the Islands. Cass helped pack boxes and boxes of food that were carried down to the port and sent off on the Island's own ships to the poorer islands.

And then one day, news came that the pirates had attacked a village on the nearby Island of Tali. Lady Sigh immediately dispatched a boat full of food, tents, building materials and helpers. Cass was among those who volunteered to go and she was never to forget the acrid stench of smoke that travelled across the water as the boat sailed into the little harbour, or the scene of complete devastation that greeted them. The pirates had set fire to every building and all that remained were the smoking, charred skeletons. Some of the people were trying to begin to repair the damage, others just stood there weeping or silently bewildered.

One elderly man, his eyes wide with shock and

grief, grabbed Cass's arm, saying, "Why did they do this? We are peaceful people. Why?" But she had no answers for him.

Cass, along with the others, stayed for a couple of weeks in Tali, helping to rebuild the village, and by the time they left, some of the physical damage had been rectified. But how long would it take for the villagers to trust strangers again, Cass wondered, and not feel a stab of fear every time a large boat pulled into its tiny harbour.

It was not long after she returned from Tali that something happened that was to change everything.

Late one evening, as Cass was walking back from helping in the infirmary, one of Lady Sigh's messengers ran up to her, saying, "Lady Sigh wants to see you now in her study."

Cass thanked her and changed direction, walking towards the circular house, wondering what the reason for the summons could be.

She knocked on the door and opened it,

expecting to see Lady Sigh sitting behind her desk in a fug of incense, poring over her papers as usual. But she was perched on a sofa by the window with Pela and another woman, who got up as soon as she walked in.

"Cass!" she cried, coming towards her. It took Cass a few seconds to realize the woman was Elsba, for she held herself so differently from how Cass remembered. And her clothes were not the dull, washed-out browns and greys that she had worn on the boat, but a scarlet-coloured shirt, a blue silk waistcoat and elegantly cut breeches. There were gold rings in her ears and her hair was braided. Even her manner was different – her shyness had disappeared. She drew Cass into a warm embrace.

"I'm so pleased to see you safe and well after all the terrible things that happened on the Palace Ship."

Through a haze of surprise, Cass agreed how lucky she had been. She felt slightly sheepish at the memory Elsba must have of her skipping off there. What a fool she had been.

"What are you doing here?" Cass asked. It

was so strange to see Elsba in the flesh, having thought of her often over the previous months.

"I am here to discuss something with you actually," she replied.

"Come and sit down," Lady Sigh said, leading the way back to the sofa and chairs by the window.

Cass followed them, her brain fizzing with curiosity, wondering what Elsba could want to talk to her about.

When they had all sat down, Elsba began, "As you know, Cass, the pirates' reign of terror in the Mid and Far Isles is growing, and there is still no sign of Enzo and Rip. Something needs to be done to stop Varen and his men but it has proved incredibly difficult for the Minarian Navy to catch them. Varen has wisely invested in the fastest ships and an impressive communication network of birds, as well as buying the tongues of the innkeepers in every port and the Mayors of most of the Islands, which all ensures that wherever the Naval fleet is, the pirates are not. So a different approach is needed. A quiet approach."

Cass nodded and Elsba went on. "Now, you

cannot hope to kill all the pirates quietly, but what you can do is cut off the head of the snake, as it were. Varen and his lieutenants need to be stopped. But how?"

Cass couldn't resist saying, with pretend innocence, "Perhaps by the Company of Eight?" and she raised an eyebrow at Elsba, who, along with Lady Sigh, stared at her in amazement.

Lady Sigh was the first to recover.

"How do you know Elsba's with the Company?" she asked.

"I guessed you were something more than a midwife after that fight in Loutrekia," Cass said to Elsba. "And then I saw your figure of eight tattoo at the baths, by accident," she added, "and when I visited Mele's house in Tarn, I put two and two together."

"I'd better be more careful in future," Elsba replied with an amused frown. "Well, you have just saved me a long explanation so I can just say briefly that I, along with five of my companions, have been tracking Varen and his four lieutenants for the last few months with as little success as the Navy. Three of the Company are now in the Far Isles, where Varen and all but two of his lieutenants are chasing a merchant's ship, but I have remained in this part of the Mid Isles, with another member, pursuing one of Varen's lieutenants, a man named Mercer.

"I have to admit that I've had little success – I have come close to him a couple of times, but he has always escaped me at the last minute. What I really need is a pair of eyes on the pirate boat. That is obviously impossible but I think I may have found the next best thing. I recently discovered that Mercer has a twin sister, called Sofia. They are close and he never goes more than a month or so without visiting her. She is an acrobat on the Circus Boat. So, Cass, that is where I hope you might come in."

"Would you like me to be your eyes, your spy, on the Circus Boat?" Cass asked, her heart jumping.

"I certainly would," Elsba replied with a laugh. "I need someone to befriend Sofia and find out as much information about her brother as possible. I know he writes to her and sends her birds, and as I said, every month or so, he comes to see her, wherever the Circus Boat is at that time. Pela tells me that you easily have the necessary skills in acrobatics, and I think you would make a good spy with a little instruction. Look at how you discovered that I was part of the Company," she said with a smile. "But you should only do this if you want to, Cass. You must not feel under any obligation. No one will think the worse of you if you say no."

"Elsba is right, Cass," Lady Sigh said. "You can still stick to your original plan of staying here and then travelling back to Minaris in a few weeks' time."

"But how do you know that Ravellous will take me on?" Cass asked. "He doesn't usually recruit anyone except in Minaris."

"I have spoken to him, and like most Islanders, he wants to do anything he can to help get rid of the pirates. He has agreed to hold sham auditions in Villuvia."

"Would you like some time to think about it?" Lady Sigh asked.

Images of Varen and the devastation at Tali flitted across Cass's brain.

"No, I don't need any time – I want to help defeat the pirates. And I have always dreamed, as you know, of performing on the Circus Boat. But what about Kov and Varen? They know me," she said. The thought of coming across either of them terrified her.

"I am confident they are miles away," Elsba replied. "Mercer's crew is the same one he's had for the last year – I have checked – so there's no one from Varen's or Kov's boat who might recognize you. And don't worry, Cass, one of us will be keeping an eye on the Circus Boat, waiting for Mercer, and if you need help, it will come."

Cass nodded, digesting all that had been said. After a moment's consideration she said, "In that case, I very much want to help."

For the next two weeks Cass was excused all other work and did nothing but train with Pela and Elsba. It was physically and mentally exhausting. They not only practised acrobatics and fighting of all types – sword and hand-to-hand combat – but Elsba also talked to Cass about everything from how to befriend Sofia, to rehearsing Cass's cover story. After much deliberation they settled on the name Ana, and, to keep things as simple as possible, decided that she should be an Island orphan.

Elsba also taught Cass how to control her anxiety and nerves, to still her mind and to focus on the matter in hand. She explained to Cass that, if she needed to, she could contact her or a member of the Company by leaving a message at one of the Postage Offices en route. She was to address it to Beatrice Holland and Elsba told her what words to use so as not to arouse suspicions were her letters to be read. Every night Cass went to bed with her brain humming and a new bruise, and she was so stiff and sore in the morning that even getting out of bed was agony. But she could feel it paying off – her balance and strength were excellent and her mind felt focused and sharp.

The day before Cass was due to leave came the moment she had been dreading. Elsba and Lady Sigh both considered that her hair was so distinctive that it must be changed. So Elsba sat her down in the herb garden behind the apothecary and before Cass knew what had happened, she had cut off her hair to just above her shoulders. Cass tried not to cry as she saw her beautiful blond hair lying around her on the floor. Then Elsba covered her remaining hair with a muddy-smelling potion.

"Come and sit in the sun – it will make it work better," she instructed.

They sat together on a small wooden bench surrounded by flowers and buzzing bees.

"I am going to leave tonight, to travel north, following up on a tip-off that Mercer is chasing a consignment of silk headed for Minaris. But don't worry, my friend Ada will be watching the Circus Boat, and whether I find Mercer or not I will meet you in Parma in two weeks' time, on the afternoon before the Circus's first street show. If you walk up from the harbour and cross a small square you will find a narrow lane known as Washing Alley – it is where all the laundries are. Look for one at the very end called Noni's.

She is a friend and has a room where we can talk."

They washed the mud out of Cass's hair and dried it with a towel. Elsba held up a hand mirror for Cass to see the result. Her hair had turned to a dull brown frizz, but Cass saw that, combined with her tanned skin, she looked remarkably different from the pale Minarian that she had been.

Elsba left that night. Cass and Pela were to sail on a fishing boat at dawn the following day so Cass said her farewells after supper.

"Well, goodbye, my friend," Annabella said to Cass, holding out her arms. "Just promise you will come back and see us, even when you are a famous acrobat."

"I promise," she said, holding Annabella close. "And in the meantime, please, please write. And look after Von for me."

"Of course, but I can predict he will be inconsolable," said Annabella with a sigh. "Are you sure they would not like a Circus cat? He has the perfect raffish look for the job."

Cass laughed. "You are right, he does. If it is allowed, I will send for him or, failing that, pick him up in a year when I return to Villuvia."

Lady Sigh jumped up from her desk, smiling broadly when Cass came to see her.

"I must give you something before you go, Cass," she said, opening a drawer and pulling out two gold citizen necklaces, one Minarian, with a small fish charm hanging off it, and an Island of Women one, like Rip had had, with a butterfly. Lady Sigh handed them both to her, explaining, "Before I knew of Elsba's plans I wrote to the city clerks in Minaris to tell them that your fish necklace had been stolen and they sent me a new one, but obviously you will now need to hide it and wear this Island one instead, as you are pretending to be an Island orphan."

Cass thanked Lady Sigh warmly. Much to her embarrassment, she had to blink back a few tears as Lady Sigh embraced her saying, "Dear Cass, I shall miss you and you must remember that there will always be a home here for you here on the Island if you want. But in the meantime, stay safe and I hope the Circus Boat brings you all the adventure that you desire."

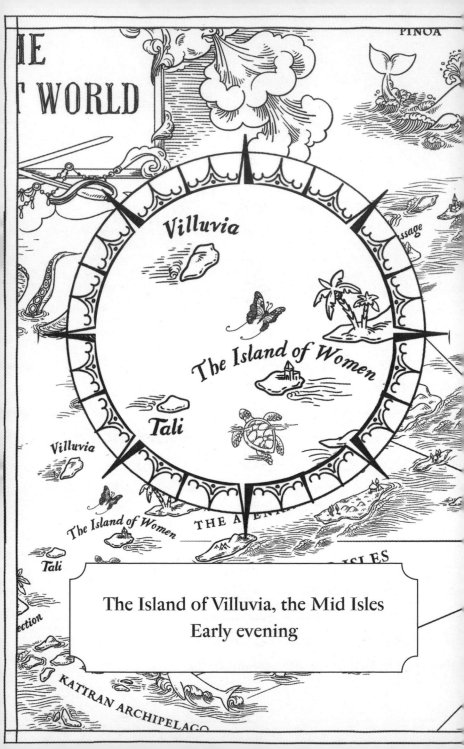

THE
T WORLD

PINOA

Villuvia

The Island of Women

Tali

Villuvia

The Island of Women

THE A

Tali

ISLES

KATIRAN ARCHIPELAGO

The Island of Villuvia, the Mid Isles
Early evening

XIV

Ravellous's Domain

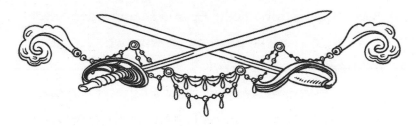

As at Minaris, Ravellous had decided to turn the auditions in Villuvia into a spectacle. Thick blue mats had been laid over the stone quay in front of the Circus Boat, and a tightrope and trapeze had been rigged up. The crowd was oohing and aahing as they watched the hopeful acrobats try out. To Cass, who had imagined this audition for so long, it seemed as if she were in a dream.

As soon as Ravellous saw Pela and Cass, he came straight over. He kissed Pela's hand playfully, saying, "Ah, the beautiful Pela, why are you still hiding away on that Island of yours? Will you not come and join us instead? I would give you star billing."

Pela smiled graciously.

"Helene would not like that," she replied. "And besides, Ravellous, as you know, I like a quiet life. This is Ana."

"Ah yes." And he held out his hand. Cass shook it as confidently as possible. "You have your father's eyes – I knew him well," he said in an undertone.

"Really?" Cass replied in a whisper, her face lighting up.

"Of course," Ravellous said softly. "Everyone knew him – he was one of the finest acrobats in the Longest World. Now, young lady, show me what you can do."

Still smiling, Cass took her place at the corner of the mats and performed her audition piece of jumps, backbends, pikes, splits and aerial somersaults, much to the delight of the crowd. She then moved on to the tightrope and trapeze – these too went smoothly and earned her more applause and whooping. To Cass it was over almost as soon as it had begun and she stood on the side, watching the other girls.

There were only a few more tryouts and when they were finished, Ravellous asked them to form a line. Cass found her stomach bubbling with nerves, despite knowing that she would be picked.

"So, as you are aware, I can only take one of you. I will put you out of your misery quickly and say that my choice, and I think the crowd's too, is Ana," he said, holding out his hand to Cass.

The crowd did indeed applaud loudly and Cass made a deep theatrical curtsy to them.

"Well done," Ravellous whispered to her out of the corner of his mouth. "You are very good – I would have taken you anyway."

Cass thanked him, grinning, and pushing any thought out of her mind other than, *It has happened, I am to be an acrobat on the Circus Boat!*

After Cass and Pela had said their goodbyes, Ravellous took Cass onboard the Circus Boat, talking incredibly quickly as he always did.

"You will sleep on the boat, and I will give you all your food and costumes and three silvers a week. We have to be back in Minaris for the King's wedding in two and a half months' time so we will limit ourselves to street shows and only raise the tent in Sedoor and Ror on the way back.

"You will be in all the shows – both in the tent and in the street performances. So that means taking part in the opening and the finale, and then a balancing act with three other acrobats – Char, Bassa and Sofia. In the tent shows, I also want you to perform in Helene's multi-trapeze act, partnering Bassa. Does that make sense so far?"

Cass nodded.

"Very good. Now, you are in luck because I am giving everyone a little holiday and there isn't a proper street show until Parma, so you have two weeks to learn the opening, the finale and the first act from the others. And then you will have to learn the trapeze act too before we reach Sedoor, which is the next time we will raise the tent. Is that understood?"

"It is," Cass replied, thinking two weeks didn't sound terribly long.

"Good, now come and let me introduce you to everyone," Ravellous said.

The boat was to set sail later that day so everyone was busy with the preparations. For Cass it was really just a blur of names and faces, except for Helene and the girls who she was to be performing with – Char, Bassa and of course Sofia. Cass was careful to pay each of them an equal amount of attention, and not seem overly curious to meet Sofia, who was sitting on her own in a quiet corner of the deck, sewing beads on to a costume. She didn't know quite what she expected the sister of a pirate to be like, but it certainly wasn't the softly spoken, shy girl who took Cass's hand politely, and said, her large brown eyes swivelling to the floor to avoid Cass's, that she hoped Cass would be happy on board. Even her face was quietly pretty, with smooth brown skin and delicate features.

Cass felt a pinch of concern that such a shy person might be difficult to get to know. But despite her misgivings, it felt good to be back on board a boat. As they cleared the harbour of Villuvia and set off towards the Island of Consta, Cass felt a bubble of excitement.

However, it had to be said that the Circus Boat made even *The Joyful Endeavour* look luxurious.

Cass now understood the significance of Ravellous saying that she would be sleeping on board. With the exception of the star performer, Helene, all the female acrobats were crammed into a single cabin for the rare nights when they were at sea, which was a claustrophobically small space lined with bunk beds and crammed full of overflowing trunks and boxes. But whenever the boat stopped at a port, however tiny, all but the lowliest of the acrobats and the circusters grabbed their bags and set off to one of the boarding houses that Ravellous had commandeered. There they could luxuriate in sleeping in a proper bed, in a room with open windows that could capture some of the night breeze, while Cass, who was most definitely one of the lowliest, was left on board with three other girls, including Sofia, to try and sleep in the sweltering cabin.

She quickly realized that the boat had a hierarchy stricter than the court at Minaris. At the top was Ravellous and his queen, Helene, who had what would be described in a romantic novel as a "stormy" relationship. When they adored each other all was rosy, but then there would be a stupendous row about something trivial. Helene would sulk and pout, Ravellous would stomp about shouting at everyone until they inevitably made it up, with much kissing and declarations of eternal love, and the whole boat would breathe a sigh of relief until the next time.

Every queen needs some ladies in waiting and admirers, and these were the next level down – the experienced acrobats, the jugglers and fire-eaters, and the musicians, the twenty or so men and women who were the glue of the show, the bulk of the company. They all flitted around Ravellous and Helene, vying for their attention and mostly ignored the likes of Cass, except to tease and reprimand, or to show off to.

Cass spent almost all her time with Char, Bassa and Sofia. Cass found Bassa by far the easiest to be with; she was a good-natured girl from the Far Isles, who moved through life easily, with a kind word for everyone. In their first rehearsal, Cass could see that she wasn't a brilliant acrobat but very strong and dependable, with a dogged diligence that meant she was perfect as a support for more gifted acrobats, like Char and Sofia. Cass was intrigued to see that Sofia, so mild in normal life, was completely fearless as an acrobat.

It was Bassa who helped Cass make her costume – Ravellous had given Cass a few bolts of material and a jar of trimmings and told her to get on with it – and the pair spent a good deal of time together, sitting on deck under the canopy. Sofia sometimes sat with them, but despite Cass's best efforts, she seldom joined in their conversations, even if she too was sewing. More often than not she would read a book, or simply stare out to sea, lost in her own thoughts. Cass found this exasperating but she hid her frustration well, careful not to arouse any sort of suspicion.

Then there was Char. Char was a tiny ball of jittery, chatty nervous energy. Cass could see that the older acrobats found her incredibly annoying, but Char was drawn to them like an irritating dog that everyone kicks but who keeps going back for more in the vain hope that she will be stroked instead. She was a fair Northerner, with straggly blond hair, an upturned nose and a thin wiry body.

Every evening, when the boat moored for the night either in the shelter of a bay or at one of the tiny, sleepy ports that lined the way, Cass and the others would make their way on shore, and find a quiet spot to practise. It was hard but the others were patient with her and after a week Cass felt that she had got the routines. But for the second act, where she would be up on the trapeze in the tent, proper rehearsals would only take place when the tent was up in Sedoor, and Helene and the others weren't going to waste their time practising with Cass, so it fell to kind Bassa to teach her this too. After they had worked on the first act, they would come back on board and loop a trapeze over the special bars that Ravellous had attached to the mast. Bassa would go through the moves with her while Ravellous, if he wasn't drinking at a quayside inn, or flirting with Helene, would wander past and cast a critical eye over Cass's practising.

As the boat drew nearer to Parma, where Cass was to meet up with Elsba, she grew increasingly alarmed at her lack of progress in finding out anything at all about Mercer. She tried to engineer being on her own with Sofia as much as possible, and told her endless made-up tales of the Island of Women, and then tried to get Sofia to talk about her own childhood and family. But it didn't work. Sofia just listened politely to Cass, smiling where she was supposed to and answered Cass's questions as briefly as she could. And then changed the subject. Always.

"...so do you have any brothers and sisters?" Cass would ask.

"Hmm, yes, a brother," Sofia would reply. "Now tell me if you think this stitching is straight."

"Yes, that looks perfect to me. So is your brother an acrobat too?"

"Oh no, nothing like that. And the trimming for this dress, do you think it should match the green? Or contrast? I really cannot decide which would be better."

"Contrast, I think. So is your brother older or younger?"

"Oh, he's my twin. Yes, I think you are right about the trimming..."

It wasn't until the day before they arrived that Mercer's name was even mentioned.

It was late afternoon and all four girls were sitting together on the boat. It was slowly pulling into the harbour of a neighbouring island, when a messenger bird fluttered down to the ship and landed at Sofia's feet. She crouched down and carefully unhooked the canister from it and walked a little way away to read the message.

Char gave a gasp of excitement and turning to Bassa, exclaimed, "Do you think it is from him? Do you think it's a message from Mercer?"

Bassa laughed and hushed her.

"Sofia has a twin brother called Mercer, who Char is sweet on," she explained in an undertone to Cass.

"He is the best-looking man in the whole of the Longest World," Char said longingly.

"Really? How exciting!" Cass replied with a casual laugh, while thinking, *This is my opportunity. I have to take it.* "When do I get to meet him?"

The girls exchanged glances, and then Bassa said, "Maybe soon. To be honest, we never know. He just appears every couple of months, and will usually take a room at an inn, and then invite us all for dinner. If Sofia has received a bird then it probably means that he will come to the show in Parma. But don't ask Sofia – she won't like it."

And as Sofia walked back, they all went back to their sewing as if the conversation had never taken place.

The Circus Boat pulled into the pretty harbour at Parma at lunchtime the following day. To Cass's relief, Ravellous gave everyone a couple of hours off before preparations for the show that night began. She grabbed a pile of her dirty clothes and told Bassa that she was off to find a laundry.

Trying to look as natural as possible, she sauntered off the ship and, following Elsba's instructions, walked through the streets away from the harbour and found Washing Alley, heavy with steamy air and the smell of soap suds, and wet sheets hung across it like flags. It was noisy too, with the sounds of women singing and shouting to each other. Halfway along was a copper sign saying *Noni's*. Cass went in and was greeted by a large lady with an open, amused face, who, when she said her name, took her washing and showed her to a small room at the back of the house. Elsba was there, ironing some clothes.

"I thought I would give Noni a hand while I waited," she explained with a laugh. "So how is everything?" she asked, shutting the door behind Cass.

"Good," Cass replied. "And I think that Mercer is coming here, tonight, to see the show!" Then she told her about the messenger bird for Sofia, and Cass's conversation with Bassa and Char.

Cass could see Elsba was gripped with excitement by the news.

"Well done, Cass, for finding that out!" she said. " I must make a plan. You say that he usually takes a room at an inn to entertain Sofia and her friends? The Inn of the Loafing Crab is the finest, so I bet it will be there…"

"Can I do anything to help?" Cass asked.

"No," Elsba replied, "you have done more than enough. Go back to the boat, prepare for the show and act normally. If by any chance you accompany Sofia to the inn tonight, do not look for me. If you happen to see me, pretend you don't know me."

Cass nodded. She felt shot through with nervous excitement at the thought of the evening and all it might bring.

The performance began at sunset and in the hours before, all the townspeople brought their chairs and jostled and squabbled about who should sit where. As the light faded, the anticipation built until Ravellous gave his sign for the show to begin. The band struck up their opening music, and the performers walked slowly from the boat to the stage, their bright costumes covered in dark cloaks, their faces obscured by masks, in a candle-lit procession. They formed a ring, facing out to the audience and Helene began her song. *It works nearly as well as in the tent*, Cass thought, watching the audience's rapt faces. And then the tempo of the music changed and everyone flung off their dark cloaks, revealing the glittering costumes beneath.

Cass's balancing act was at the end of the

programme, so she withdrew to the neighbouring building which Ravellous had commandeered, and watched out of a window while the jugglers and fire-eaters took to the stage. She could feel her performance nerves building so she tried to focus instead on scanning the audience, trying to guess who Mercer was. She had come up with a few likely candidates when Helene took to the stage for her ribbon act. It was a testament to how amazing she was, Cass thought, that although the audience could see the men pulling the rope of ribbon up and down, that did not seem to detract in any way from the magic of it. They just saw Helene soaring up and down, letting the ribbon lift her, playing with it as if it were another person, twirling and turning on it until their heads were giddy with watching.

Cass was so mesmerized she forgot to feel nervous and it was almost a surprise when Char said to her, "Come on, it is us now."

Like the other three girls, Cass's hair was pulled back tightly in a bun and her face obscured with a mask. They all wore matching red outfits, with stiff skirts designed to look like flower petals, so that only the difference in skin tone of the girls' arms and legs distinguished them and the act was designed around this. They started lying in a star shape waving their arms in time to the music and then quickly went into various balances. The act had been beautifully worked out, playing to each girl's strength, and the super bendy, light Char was almost always on the top of the contortions, with Bassa at the bottom holding everyone else up. The slow, rhythmic dance music and the costumes were perfect and the audience, still buoyed up by Helene, adored it. Cass felt giddy with relief when it was over and the audience were applauding and noisily catcalling. It was after they had taken their bows at the end that Sofia caught her arm.

"Ana," she said in her soft voice, "my brother wishes to meet you." And Cass found herself face to face with a young man. He was indeed good-looking and dressed like a young prince, with fat gold chains hanging round his neck. Cass could sense she was being inspected and felt herself flush slightly with nerves.

"I have taken a room at the inn over there. I would appreciate you joining us for dinner," Mercer said, with the air of a man used to giving orders.

Cass nodded. She gathered that he had already invited Bassa and Char, and sure enough they were busy getting changed back at the boat. Char was in a state of high excitement, having changed into her skimpiest dress, and was piling on jewellery and face rouge. It was the very opposite of Sofia's outfit, which Cass noticed was a very modest, high-necked dress in a dull-coloured silk. Cass had nothing but the shirts and breeches that she wore every day but as she started to put on the cleanest of them, Sofia noticed and said, "Oh no, please let me lend you something to wear."

"Don't worry," Cass said. "I don't mind."

"No, but my brother will," she said, looking anxious. "He cannot bear a woman to wear breeches. Please borrow one of my dresses. Please, it will be easier for me."

Cass had a sudden urge to plead a headache and avoid the evening all together, but she knew she should go to see if she could glean any more information. So she smiled brightly and said, "Of course," and took the mud-coloured dress that Sofia held out to her.

The Inn of the Loafing Crab,
the Island of Parma, the Northern Mid Isles
Eight o'clock in the evening

XV

A Bag of Buns

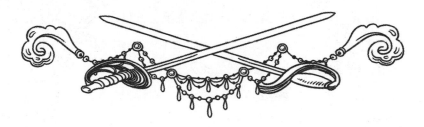

The inn was dark and smoky. Cass focused on looking straight ahead and breathing deeply to calm the nerves that were now bubbling up in her stomach. Everything felt suddenly very real and her mind kept flashing up images of Kov and Varen. *Stop it!* she told herself strictly. *He does not know you. Breathe and act naturally.* As they were led up some stairs, she thought she saw Elsba out of the corner of her eye and quickly looked away.

They were shown into a dining chamber on the first floor, with windows on all three sides obscured by netting to stop the insects. Cass could hear the large island moths blundering against them. The room was brightly lit with an extravagant number of candles and the table was laid with silver cutlery and expensively painted plates.

Mercer was sitting at the end of the table, smoking a cigarillo and drinking a glass of thick red wine. He jumped up when they appeared and kissed Sofia on each cheek. He held her back for inspection, saying, "You look tired. Is Ravellous working you too hard?"

"No, not at all," Sofia replied quickly as he helped her to a seat next to his, and the others sat down around the table, Char making sure that she sat on Mercer's other side.

Plates of food were brought and everyone began to help themselves, except Sofia, Cass noticed. She waited for Mercer to serve her, which he did, considering each dish before spooning it on to her plate. He was asking her questions in a low voice, and Cass tried to catch what he was saying while pretending not to. It sounded as if he was mostly asking about her performance, and whether she would soon have her own act.

Cass could also see that Char was desperate to engage Mercer's attention. But it was to Cass that Mercer turned his focus next.

"So, Ana," he began, "you are new to the boat, my sister tells me."

"Yes," Cass replied. "I joined at Villuvia."

"Where are you from?" Mercer asked.

"The Island of Women. I'm an Island orphan," said Cass, showing him her citizen necklace.

"Really?" Mercer said, pausing for a moment, as if a bell had just rung at the back of his head. "An acrobat from the Island of Women," he repeated, looking at her closely. Cass could begin to feel her palms sweat, though she kept her face calm as Elsba had taught her.

"Why?" she asked lightly, a questioning smile on her face, her tone playful. "Is that such a strange thing?"

"No," Mercer said, his eyes still fully focused on her. "It's just there was a Minarian girl, who my boss was looking for last year. She was an acrobat on her way to the Island of Women."

"Oh," Cass replied as innocently as she could. "Well, she never arrived. I was the only acrobat there. Could you pass me the beans, please?" she asked Bassa, her stomach churning.

"Of course," Bassa replied. "Wasn't Sofia brilliant tonight at the end?" she said to Mercer.

"Of course, she is the best," he replied and they all laughed and the moment passed.

"You should see her in our new tent act," Char said eagerly. "Will you come and watch our first performance in Sedoor next week?"

"Sadly I cannot," Mercer replied. "My work will take me over to the Far Isles for several weeks. And by the time I am finished there you will be nearly at Minaris, so I will wait until you return to the Mid Isles."

"What a shame," Char replied, her face falling.

Cass felt her nerves subside a little as Char chattered on, and she forced herself to finish her meal and smile brightly at the conversation. Mercer seemed mostly focused on Sofia, but every so often he glanced over at Cass, with a look in his eyes that suggested something about her would not settle in his mind. Cass did her best to ignore this and despite her jangling nerves, she managed to say goodbye and thank

Mercer prettily at the end of the evening. She chatted to the other girls as normally as she could as they walked back to the boat, thinking she had never felt so relieved to get an evening over in her life.

"Isn't he handsome?" Char said, dancing along in front of them.

Cass made herself smile and laugh. "I can see why you like him," she replied.

"It was kind of him to take us to dinner," Cass said to Sofia.

Sofia hesitated and then made what seemed to Cass a strange reply.

"Oh, Ana," she said. "Do not think kindness had anything to do with it."

Let Elsba capture Mercer tonight, Cass prayed, as she lay wide awake in the sweltering heat of the cabin while the other girls slept around her. *Let him be safely in chains by tomorrow.* He had clearly suspected her, but was it enough for him to do anything about it? she wondered.

She must have dropped off because she woke up in the morning to find the cabin empty. She dressed and washed at top speed and made her way up to the deck. Char, Bassa and Sofia were in a gaggle. Sofia had her back to Cass, but the other two were looking alarmed and Bassa had her hand on Sofia's arm in a comforting way. Cass felt a lift of excitement that she was careful not to show on her face.

"Is everything all right?" she asked, her face a picture of concern.

"Someone tried to attack Sofia's brother last night as he left the inn," Char announced.

"What?" Cass raised her hand to her mouth in mock shock. "Was he harmed?"

Sofia shook her head. "Not really," she replied, her face pale. "And he has left now. I must go and get on with my sewing." And she hurried off.

"How awful for her," Cass said to the others.

Bassa nodded thoughtfully and Char babbled on. But Cass wasn't really listening, she was worrying about Elsba. She made some suitable comments, before excusing herself on the pretext of collecting her laundry.

Elsba was there, sitting in the back room. Her face was bruised and her arm in a sling, but she gave Cass a bright smile.

"I would have had him if some other men hadn't come to his aid," she said, annoyed with herself. "Next time I will get him."

"He has gone to the Far Isles," Cass said.

"Really!" Elsba said, her face brightening. "Did he tell you that at dinner?"

Cass nodded.

"How was the dinner?" Elsba asked.

Cass was about to tell her about his questions, but then stopped herself. Elsba had enough to concern her, and besides, he had gone now.

"It was fine," she replied. "Uneventful and I'm afraid that was all I found out about him, except that he likes to feel in charge of Sofia."

"I can imagine," Elsba said. "Well, I will follow him over to the Far Isles. He will have to wait to see Sofia – he will not risk visiting her once they get too close to Minaris."

"Yes, that was what he said," Cass confirmed.

Elsba nodded, digesting all this information.

"He may still send her birds though, with news.

If you find out any more will you write to me – care of the Postage Office in Hendra. Thank you, Cass, for all you have done. You can breathe a little easier now and enjoy the rest of the trip."

Cass laughed.

"You are forgetting that it's my first night on the trapeze in the big tent next week in Sedoor, so that's not that relaxing," she pointed out.

"Too true," Elsba replied. "Good luck, not that you need it, I'm sure."

They wished each other goodbye and Cass picked up her clean washing before strolling back to the Circus Boat, feeling just a little sad that her small part in chasing the pirates was over.

Sedoor was situated at the head of a deep natural harbour and it was notorious for the sea fogs that swept in most evenings. It had been the old capital of the ancient kingdom of Tys, and until recently was the military base and administrative capital of the Mid Isles.

As soon as the boat docked in the harbour,

the circusters busied themselves unloading the vast blue tent and all the Circus equipment and carrying it up to the main square, which was called the Square of Dreamers. Meanwhile, the performers turned their attention to pressing and mending the costumes and props. Cass had checked all of hers, and since she still had a few hours before rehearsals began, and feeling nervous and in the way, she decided to go ashore to distract herself.

Cass's first impressions of Sedoor were bittersweet. It wasn't that she didn't like it – on the contrary she enjoyed walking along the wide streets admiring the gracious, crumbling stone buildings that lined them. And although the weather was still mild, it had lost the tropical heat, and the light was colder and clearer, illuminating everything crisply in the morning sunlight. It was just that elements of it – the swarms of wild cats and the beggars everywhere – reminded her intensely of the day she had spent in Tarn with Rip.

As much as Cass fretted over what might have happened to Lion, it was Rip who chiefly occupied her thoughts. She often talked to him in her head – funny, easy conversations that had nothing to do with pirates. But when she woke in the night, she was gripped by an intense fear that Varen had killed him and she would never see him again.

Cass walked up to the Square of Dreamers, where the tent was being raised like a great blue beast. A crowd of excited onlookers had gathered, laughing and joking and cheering as it inched up towards the sky. Cass felt a jab of nerves, as she thought how later she would be in there performing in front of hundreds of people. And before that were the rehearsals with Helene and the others. However diligently Bassa had taught her, it was not the same as performing at the top of the tent.

There was a baker's nearby oozing a mouthwateringly delicious smell of sugar and vanilla. Cass walked towards it with the intention of buying something large and sweet to devour. She nearly bumped straight into a man coming out, carrying a large bag of cakes.

"Excuse me," she said and then looked up to

see that it was Captain Bemot, the captain of *The Joyful Endeavour.*

"Cassandra?" he said. "Is that you? You look different."

"I know, I changed my hair," she replied, surprised that he had still recognized her.

"I have often wondered about you and hoped that you weren't caught up in that business with the pirates and the Palace Ship," he said. "Come, you must tell me your news. And as I've just bought too many of these buns from the bakery, will you have one to stop me eating them all? My wife says I get fatter with every voyage."

Cass said she would be delighted to and they sat down on a bench. She told him an alternative version of events, where she had left the Palace Ship in Tarn, as they had decided on a change of route, and then made her own way down to the Island of Women on another merchant's boat.

"That sounds quite the adventure," Captain Bemot said.

"Yes, it was," Cass agreed with a smile, thinking, *If you only knew the truth.*

"Anyway, tell me what brings you to Sedoor?" the captain asked.

Cass explained that she was headed back to Minaris on the Circus Boat.

Captain Bemot gasped. "Your dream came true then! Good for you, Cass! I am coming to see the show tonight and I will be sure to look out for you. I'm headed back to Minaris too, just in time for the Royal wedding – what a grand party that should be!" he said. "I have a boat full of fabric – silks and cottons from Gram – rather easier than all those goats! It makes up for the lack of passengers – no one is travelling these days because of the pirates. Personally I think it's a fuss about nothing – I haven't seen any and besides everyone says they have gone back to the Far Isles." He finished his bun and dusted the sugar off his fingers. "Well, I must be getting back to my boat," he said, standing up. "But it has been a great pleasure to see you, Cassandra. Do come and look me up in Minaris when we are back."

They shook hands warmly and Cass thanked him for the buns before she said goodbye. As she watched him go, she thought what a very nice man he was.

Four hours later, rehearsals had begun and Cass was dangling from the double trapeze with Bassa, every muscle in her body screaming as she held the difficult poses designed to frame Helene and show her off to her best. They had rehearsed the act twice already and on the first time, Cass had nearly lost her footing and it was only Bassa's strength that had saved her from tumbling down on to the net stretched out beneath them.

But since that bad start, it had gone smoothly for Cass and it was Helene who kept making mistakes. Ravellous, who was watching them, bellowed at her, making her even more clumsy and nervous. The act ended with them all dropping together down from the trapezes into the net, and Helene got her timing wrong, jumping before the others were ready. Ravellous yelled at her and, in revenge, Helene stalked up to him and slapped him hard in the face, before storming off.

Ravellous, who was by now in a terrible mood,

made Cass and the other girls repeatedly rehearse their other act, nit-picking and making endless confusing changes. He wouldn't let them go for about an hour, while his temper cooled, and the girls grew increasingly tired and exasperated. At last he was done and released them. The others went outside to sit in the sun, but Cass stayed in the tent to watch the following acts. Up next were the fire-eaters, and then Helene's solo piece followed by the juggler, Wildo.

Cass was so absorbed in watching Helene that she jumped when Char sat down beside her. She began chatting generally to Cass and then said, "So, tell me what a girl from the Island of Women is doing with a citizen necklace from Minaris?" And she dangled Cass's fish necklace from a finger in front of her face.

Cass's first thought was one of fury.

"How dare you snoop through my things!" she hissed, snatching the necklace off Char's finger.

Char shrugged, a half-smile on her face. Her eyes glittered at Cass in the darkness of the tent as she asked her, "Are you sure you're not the girl from Minaris that Mercer is looking for?"

"Positive!" Cass snapped back. "Write to Lady Sigh if you don't believe me. That necklace was my mother's – it's all I have left of her. Don't you dare touch it again." And she got to her feet, stalking off before Char could say anything else.

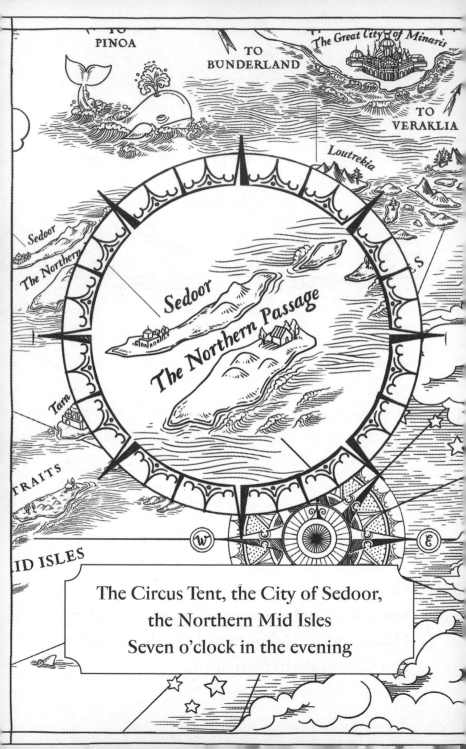

PINOA

TO
BUNDERLAND

TO
VERAKLIA

The Great City of Minaris

Loutrekia

Sedoor

The Northern

Sedoor

The Northern Passage

Tarn

STRAITS

MID ISLES

W   E

The Circus Tent, the City of Sedoor,
the Northern Mid Isles
Seven o'clock in the evening

XVI

Latecomers

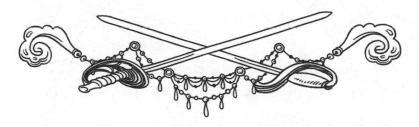

A performance in the tent was a far greater event than a street show, with a much bigger audience and many more acts and costume changes, and as a result everyone was significantly more tense. Nerves either made people silent or overly chatty, Cass observed, as they stood squashed into the backstage area, stretching and limbering up while the audience took their seats. She had deliberately positioned herself as far away from Char as possible, but she could see and hear her being noisy and annoying everyone, particularly Helene. In fact Helene looked like she wanted to slap Char, as she had Ravellous.

"It's time," Ravellous announced, poking his head around the curtain that separated the performers from the audience.

"Helene, go up to the trapeze and everyone else, light your candles. I will give you the signal. Good luck, all of you!"

He allowed Helene a few minutes to climb up the ladder to the small platform, and then when he was sure she was up there and had the trapeze, he gave the signal and the lights in the auditorium were extinguished.

The performers walked out into the dark arena, as everyone held their breath, waiting for Helene to sing. There was a long pause, and then it came – her clear voice and the single candle flame descending down. Everyone cheered as she reached the ground and the music's tempo increased. The stagehands lit the main lamps.

Cass had learned not to look too closely at the audience in case they put her off but sometimes it was impossible not to see the faces of those sitting in the front row of seats – Ravellous packed them in so closely they were practically tripping over their feet. So Cass was surprised that evening to see an empty row of seats in front of her. *Latecomers,* she thought with a performer's irritation.

"They're a great audience," Wildo announced, as he walked into the backstage area, to a chorus of cheering and clapping, his act having finished. Cass was on next with Helene and the others.

They all got into position and the music started. A few minutes into the routine, as Cass was dangling from the trapeze by her foot, holding on to one of Bassa's feet in order to make a chain, there was some movement in the audience. *Don't get distracted,* she told herself, but her eyes were irresistibly drawn to what was going on. *It's the latecomers,* she thought, her eyes flicking over to them. And then she felt her stomach plummet, as she recognized Mercer. And even worse, swaggering along next to him, with an air of affected nonchalance, was Kov. They were surrounded by a gang of henchmen.

It was one of the few times in her life that Cass thought she might faint. Black spots appeared in front of her eyes and her hands grew slippery with sweat. Her heart hammered in her chest as she tried to go through the motions of her part. *What were they doing there?* Her brain was spinning. Bassa gave her a sharp prod with her foot as if to say "what are you doing?" So Cass tried to focus but she couldn't stop looking at the pirates. What if Kov recognized her? *Don't look*, she told herself, *you are wearing a mask.*

Cass was so distracted that she missed a cue and failed to hold Bassa's trapeze tightly enough, and as a result Bassa nearly fell, and only just managed to clumsily right herself. She shot Cass a furious look, which made Cass pull herself together, and somehow she got through the rest of the act.

"What happened to you?" Helene hissed as they walked out of the ring. "Sort yourself out!"

"Bassa, I am so sorry," Cass apologized as soon as it was over.

Bassa looked at her with a withering expression that Cass had never seen on her kind, gentle face. "Don't ever let it happen again," she replied.

Cass sat down on her own in the corner of the changing area. *Why were they here?* Her brain started spinning – had Char tipped Mercer off about her fish necklace? And had he brought Kov to identify her? Panic rose in her stomach and she could hear Elsba telling her to breathe, just breathe and don't let your imagination run away with you. You don't know any of this. It is more likely that Mercer perhaps had a change of plan and decided to come to see Sofia, and Kov happened to be here too. She would keep her mask on and Kov would not know her – how could he?

"We're on, Ana!" Sofia called to her, and Cass walked out into the arena with the others.

Afterwards, Cass would never know how she got through not only her act but also the finale. Her sole comfort was that whenever she stole a glance at Mercer and Kov, their attention seemed to be fully focused on Sofia or Helene.

As Cass walked backstage, she felt some measure of relief. She would pretend she had a headache and then after a quick trip to the Postage Office, she would go straight back to the boat, and there she would stay all day tomorrow and the next day except for the performances. And she would just have to pray that Char had swallowed the story of the fish necklace belonging to her mother.

Char, Bassa and Sofia were in a gaggle, and Cass, trying to act as normally as possible, went straight up to them.

"Your brother is here. That is a nice surprise for you," she said to Sofia.

Sofia nodded, but it was Char who seemed excited.

"Do you think he will take us out tonight?" she asked breathlessly.

Before Sofia could respond, Cass told them about her headache and said that she was going straight back to the boat and wished them a good night.

She put her head round the curtain, just to check that the audience had left the tent before she went too. But to her horror she saw Ravellous was talking to Kov and Mercer. Despite the ingratiating smile pinned to his face, Ravellous looked very nervous, almost fearful. They all turned towards Cass, who shot back like a scalded cat and slid behind the changing screen.

She watched surreptitiously as the three men came around the curtain. Ravellous cleared his throat for silence and introduced them respectfully, adding that Mercer was, of course, Sofia's brother, and Cass saw Helene and a couple of the older performers stiffen.

"Thank you all for a marvellous show," Kov said smoothly.

The sound of his voice made Cass's head swim and she had to fight back the vivid memories of that terrible night, which were flooding her brain. *I always catch my prey, Cassandra.*

"Thank you so much," Ravellous said to Kov, turning to the rest of them. "I am also incredibly honoured to tell you that these gentlemen have asked for some of you perform on their boss's boat at a special private show tomorrow evening."

Boss! He must mean Varen, Cass thought, her heart tumbling and her legs feeling as if they might give way. But she tried to keep listening to what was being said.

"We will delay our normal show as it really is such a great honour," Ravellous repeated, licking his lips nervously. "So, Helene, of course, you will go." Helene smiled politely and gave a slight bow, and then focused her gaze on the floor to avoid meeting anyone's eye. "And I understand you wanted Wildo, the juggler."

Wildo, who clearly knew exactly who Kov and Mercer were, quickly said, "Of course, sires, I would be honoured."

"And the fire-eaters," Kov went on, looking around at everyone. "I am sure they will amuse him." He paused. "And we must have the beautiful Sofia and her friends."

"Absolutely," Ravellous replied and, behind the screen, Cass thought she might be sick.

Cass hardly slept that night. After the show, she had dashed through the streets to the Postage Office. She sent a message by bird to the Postage Office in Hendra to alert Elsba, although she knew it was almost impossible that she would have reached there already. And then, despite knowing that no one was likely to pick it up, she left a message addressed to Beatrice Holland, saying, *Please send more wool for knitting*, which was the Company's code for an emergency. In desperation she added, *All the children have returned home to me — there is a great celebration on their boat near Sedoor tomorrow night. I do so hope you can make it.* And then she sprinted back to the boat, climbed into her hammock and tried to decide, as calmly as she could, what to do.

In many ways, the choice seemed easy. She had done all she could to alert the Company to the pirates' presence, and now she had to consider her own safety. She was sure that Captain Bemot would take her back to Minaris. There was the slight matter of her lack of silvers but she would just have to get a job as soon as she arrived to pay for the cost of her passage, which seemed a small price for avoiding the pirates. The thought of Captain Bemot's battered boat filled Cass with such nostalgia that she felt almost homesick for it. She could leave a note for Ravellous, and Cass was certain he would understand and allow her back into the Circus later. So that, surely, was what she should do?

But, a voice nagged in her head, *what about Rip?* If Varen was there, then Rip and Enzo, if they were still alive, were likely to be with him too. Cass didn't particularly care about Enzo but Rip had risked his life to help her, so shouldn't she do the same? Or at the very least find out if he was alive. She also had an overwhelming urge to see him again. But what about the danger to her life? Would Kov or Varen recognize her wearing a mask? She knew that if they did, they would kill her. And there was also the question of Char – would she have told Mercer or Kov about the fish necklace? If she hadn't already, she might have done that night.

The questions and arguments bounced back and forth, to and fro, like a ball trapped in her head, until finally she fell asleep for a couple of hours at dawn as the others came in from the party.

When Cass woke up she had decided. The other girls were still sleeping, so she dressed quietly and crept out on to the deserted deck, and sped down on to the quay. She hoped it was too early for the pirates to be about, but she still felt nervous and walked hurriedly along under the colonnade, swivelling to look in the shop windows if anyone passed her. She caught sight of *The Joyful Endeavour* moored at the other end of the harbour, and headed towards it. But when she had almost reached the boat, she turned away from the quay and up a side street, to make her preparations.

"How can I help you, miss?" the man in the knife shop said. He had a patronising look about him, Cass thought, as if he imagined a girl would know nothing about weapons.

"May I see those two daggers, please?" she asked, pointing to his display. "And also that one with the very narrow blade?"

The man smiled as he laid them out on the counter.

"Are you buying a present for your brother? Or perhaps a friend?"

"No, it's for me," Cass replied coolly, weighing each knife in her hand, checking the weight and the grip. *It should feel like an extension of your hand,* Pela had said. They were all good but the one with the narrow blade was smaller and more discreet.

"Can I see the sheath for the narrow one please?"

The man produced a sturdy-looking leather sheath. Cass examined it, thinking carefully. It would just fit in the pocket of her cloak, she decided.

"Yes, I will take it," she said to the man and paid him the three silvers he wanted.

You must always name a weapon, Pela had said. *Give it the name of someone whose characteristics you want it to have.* Cass wanted the knife to be dependable, loyal and hard-working. *I name you Tig,* she said to the knife before she carefully hid it in her clothes.

They set off at seven that evening, just as some light fog was rolling in off the sea. In the early afternoon, Cass had watched as the Mayor of Sedoor had stormed on to the deck of the ship, furious that the show was cancelled until Ravellous explained the reason. Then his eyes grew wide, saying of course Ravellous must do everything he could to keep the pirates happy. The performers had eaten a late lunch of sorts on board the Circus Boat, but no one had much of an appetite, least of all Cass. She felt as if she were about to walk into a cave of vicious, starving bears, with only a small knife for protection.

Mercer came to collect them in a large rowing boat and, as usual, fussed over his sister. Sofia remained as calm and inscrutable as ever while Char, who Cass had successfully avoided all day, positioned herself next to Mercer. Cass tried not to feel paranoid as, out of the corner of her eye, she watched Char begin a whispered conversation with him.

It was too misty for her to see exactly where they were going, but she judged it to be to the north-west of Sedoor. They skirted around several bays until they came to one that was almost hidden from view by high cliffs. They passed through its narrow mouth and two ships loomed out of the fog. Cass could faintly hear the sound of waves breaking so she knew they couldn't be far from the shore. The rowing boat pulled up against the side of one of the ships, which was called *The Narina. I hope that is not a terrible omen*, Cass thought wryly as she twisted Lin's ring on her finger, wondering whether Lin could see what she was up to. *She would be furious*, she thought with a smile, and said a silent prayer to both Lin and her parents to help her. She pulled her mask over her face and followed the others as they climbed up the rope ladder on to the deck.

Enzo was the first person Cass saw. He was standing with Varen, laughing and joking. They were the only people on deck apart from Kov. She slid back so she was shielded from their view by Bassa and observed him surreptitiously. At first glance he looked well, but then she could see that actually he was too thin and was nervously playing with his fingers as he tried to ingratiate himself to Varen. But she couldn't bring herself to feel any pity towards him after how he had treated her. There was no sign of Rip.

Kov greeted Ravellous and introduced him to Varen. Cass could feel the sweat dripping off her as Varen came forward. But she also felt something she hadn't expected – anger.

Here was the man who had caused so much misery

to so many people and for what? Cass thought furiously. *His own greed.*

"Welcome, all of you," Varen said with his gracious, professorial air, as if he were about to give them a tour of his library. "Thank you for coming and providing me with such a delightful diversion. As you can see, I have sent all my men to the other ship in case you found them intimidating."

"How soon can you begin?" Mercer asked Ravellous.

"Almost immediately," Ravellous replied, his voice gravelly with nerves. "We just need to hook up the apparatus for Helene's act."

"Excellent," said Varen. "Kov, Mercer, please see that they have what they need. Perhaps the other performers would like to wait below deck."

To Cass's relief, Ravellous sent them down, although Sofia waited up on deck with her brother. As they stood awkwardly in the corridor, Char chattered away nervously, while Bassa was silent. The boat smelled horrible, which didn't help Cass's nervous nausea. To stop herself gagging, she covered her nose with her cloak and breathed through it, as she edged away from the group, intending to go and try to find Rip.

But then a small figure came towards her, with a mop of curly hair, his head down, walking listlessly. Before she could stop herself, she cried, "Lion!" She pulled up her mask and he raised his head, a great grin spreading across his face.

"Goatsmilk!" he replied, flinging himself at her.

Tears of happiness spilled out of Cass's eyes as she hugged him close. "What are you doing here?" she asked.

"Kov decided to take me and one of the girls, Hiva, with him from the slave ship," he paused, his face hard, unreachable. "Hiva died." Cass hugged him tight again.

"I'm so sorry," she said.

"It is not so bad, being their slave," Lion said with a shrug, but there was something in his manner that told her it was.

"Why did you dye your lion hair?" he asked.

"So they wouldn't recognize me," Cass whispered, remembering Rip. "Is Rip here? I saw Enzo on deck but not Rip."

Lion sighed. "He is, but he's very sick. They refuse to get a doctor for him so I think he may die soon," he said in a matter-of-fact way.

"Can't Enzo help?" Cass asked.

Lion gave a rude snort. "He's a pirate now," he said.

Cass desperately wanted to see Rip. She glanced back at Bassa but she and Char had their backs to her. She wondered how long she had before they had to perform. She should be fine for ten minutes, she decided.

"Can you take me to him?" she asked.

Lion nodded and produced a candle stub out of his pocket and some matches. Once it was lit, he led her down into the bowels of the ship. The smell was almost unbearable. He unbolted a door and opened it and Cass went into a tiny room, her eyes squinting with lack of light.

Rip was lying, asleep, on a pile of filthy blankets on the floor. His breathing was laboured and uneven and she could see even in the half-light that he was emaciated. She went over and touched his arm. He was boiling hot.

"Rip," she said softly. "Rip, it's me, Cass."

He stirred and opened his eyes. It took a few moments for him to recognize her.

"Cass. What are you doing here?" he said, his voice no more than a whisper.

"It's a long story," she replied, anxious about time. "I'm so sorry about your uncle."

"Thank you," he said weakly and then his body was shaken by a violent fit of coughing.

He's going to die soon, Cass thought desperately. Fear and pity stoked her fury, and she said fiercely to him, "I will get help. I will get word to the Minarian Navy – they have been looking for you frantically but everyone thinks you are in the Far Isles. They will come and get you, it will be all right."

Rip nodded, as if he didn't really believe it.

"You should go now," he said. "You shouldn't have come – if they see you they will kill you." The effort of speaking sent him off into another coughing fit.

Cass knew he was right and that she would be going to perform in a moment, but she felt she must do something for him. She pulled the knife out of her pocket and tried to give it to him so that he could defend himself.

But Rip laughed and held up his hands. They were chained.

"It will take more than a knife to get me out of here. Keep it, you may need it. Now go!" he said with one last effort.

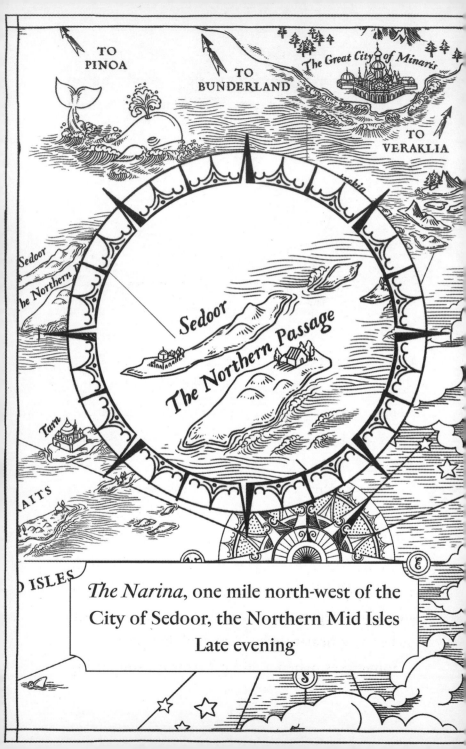

TO PINOA

TO BUNDERLAND

The Great City of Minaris

TO VERAKLIA

Sedoor

The Northern Passage

Sedoor

The Northern Passage

Tarn

AITS

ISLES

The Narina, one mile north-west of the City of Sedoor, the Northern Mid Isles
Late evening

XVII

At Last It Is Done

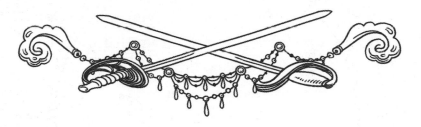

Cass only just made it back to the others in time. They were cursing her as she came up, pulling her mask down and shoving the knife back into the pocket of her cloak, which she then threw off. She followed them up the steps.

"Where were you?!" Ravellous hissed.

Cass ignored him and walked behind the others out on to the deck. Enzo was sitting next to Varen, right in front of where they were to perform. *Make me invisible*, she prayed, *make him not see me.* The musicians began the music that she knew as well as her own heartbeat and she took her place.

Sometimes, when a group performs, something

273

is wrong; perhaps someone's timing is slightly out which means it is not as slick as it could be and everything becomes a little more juddery and jolting. But occasionally everyone is in such perfect synchronicity that they move as smoothly as water running in a stream. And that show for the pirates was one of those times. It flowed beautifully, effortlessly, and a calm fell over the small audience as they watched the girls' bodies move perfectly in time to the music. Cass was completely absorbed in what she was doing, and resisted any pull to look at Varen and Enzo until the act was over. But then, as they stood in a row to take their applause, she could feel Enzo studying her. And when she flicked her eyes down to look at him, he had looked away and was whispering in Varen's ear, making Varen laugh. *Don't tell him,* she prayed. *Please, Enzo, don't tell him.*

Only Helene's act remained so Cass and the others stayed on deck, standing to one side. Cass positioned herself as far away as she could from Enzo and Varen, making sure that Bassa and the others were screening her from view. She was so distracted – thinking of how she would soon be off the boat, and that tomorrow she would send word to the Navy somehow (perhaps she should send a bird to Lady Sigh? Surely she would know how to get in contact with them?) – that she gave a start when she realized that Helene had finished. Varen had stood up and was busy applauding Helene and shaking Ravellous's hand. He stopped by Wildo and the fire-eaters and joked with them. And then he walked over towards Cass and the other girls. *Breathe*, Cass told herself, *and pretend*.

"And I have to thank you girls too for a brilliant performance," he said, taking Bassa's hand in his, and then Sofia's, and then Char's. Cass thought her heart would burst out of her chest it was hammering so hard as he moved down the line towards her. She held out her sweating hand to him.

"And you, of course," he said with a smile, taking her hand firmly in his. "The shy one on the end. I know I shouldn't have favourites but you were mine." Cass smiled as gracefully as she could. He was staring at her, still holding her hand.

"Take off your mask so I can see your face," he said to her slowly, still smiling. Cass faltered.

Everyone else was looking at her, as if to say, *take off the mask!* So, swallowing hard, she brought her free hand up to her face and pulled it off. Varen paused and pulled her close to him, as if they were about to dance.

"So sweet-looking. But you know, I believe we have met before." He paused, and moved away from her, almost as if he were about to let her go, but he didn't. He put a finger on his chin, as if he were thinking. The atmosphere on deck changed in a moment from lighthearted to tense. Kov and Mercer looked at her intently, their hands wandering towards the swords at their belts.

"I know!" Varen said, his play-acting now unmistakably tinged with menace. "It was in Tarn! Do you remember?"

Cass flicked her eyes to Char but she was looking bewildered, not guilty, so she moved her glance to Enzo. He met her eye for a second with an expression of defiant misery that said to her, *I have only done what I needed to survive.*

Well, Cass thought, *you have betrayed me twice, now I shall betray you.* A clear calm descended over her and she nodded.

"You do remember!" Varen replied. "I am so flattered. Remind me of how we met."

She opened her mouth to tell Varen how taking the necklace had been Bastien and Enzo's idea, that she had just been their pawn, but the words stuck in her throat. She realized that if she told Varen, he would kill Enzo too. And although it might be just that he should die along with her, she did not want that responsibility. So instead she said, "I tried to steal a necklace belonging to your friend Narina."

"Yes, you did. And now you will pay for it." He turned abruptly to Ravellous. "My friend, I assume you had no idea that you had employed a thief."

Cass looked at Ravellous. He was pale as milk and pouring with sweat.

"No," he replied.

"Good. Mercer, please get one of your men to escort these good people back to Sedoor."

Ravellous hesitated, looking at Cass.

"She is only a child," he managed to say. "Please let her come with us and I promise you will never see her again."

"There is no question of it," Varen replied. "Now go, before I become angry and decide that you are all to be punished."

Ravellous gave a short nod, and shut his eyes as if he were praying.

"Very well," he muttered and without looking at Cass, ushered the others to the rowing boat. Only Bassa glanced back at her, Cass noticed, with a look of sympathetic fear smeared across her face.

Varen was silent as they boarded the boat and went. Then he turned back to Cass.

"So, Cassandra the thief, what shall we do with you?" he said.

Suddenly, there was a massive explosion and a rip of splintering wood. The whole ship lurched violently to one side, separating Cass from Varen and sending everyone flying across the deck. Clouds of thick blue-grey smoke billowed through the air and there was an intense smell of burning. Cass picked herself up to find the ship tilting to one side, and a cacophony of shouting from the other ship. As the smoke cleared she could see a massive hole in the deck where Enzo and Mercer had been standing.

"We are being attacked!" Kov shouted, getting to his feet.

Cass looked at the other pirate ship. It was swarming with the bright blue uniforms of the Minarian Navy, who were fighting furiously with the pirates. It must have been one of the Navy's cannonballs that had blown a hole in the side of *The Narina*, she realized. She looked around desperately for Varen and saw him a moment later, lying unconscious on the other side of the deck. *If I get my knife, I can kill him now and then it will be over*, she thought, making a dash for the staircase that led below deck, where she had left her cloak. But Kov was too quick for her. His sword was against her throat before she could move.

"Not so fast," he said. "Please forgive me but as I have soldiers to kill I will make it quick." But as he pulled the sword back to slice through her neck, something happened. He looked at Cass with an expression of utter astonishment and dropped his weapon to the ground with a clatter. His legs buckled and he collapsed. Cass saw her dagger sticking in his back and Lion standing behind him. He calmly pulled the dagger out and wiped it on Kov's shirt, before handing it back to Cass.

"Now we have to go!" Lion said. "The ship will sink or the soldiers will come to this ship and think that we are pirates and kill us!"

Cass knew he was right but she couldn't leave yet.

"I have to get Rip first," she replied.

"No!" Lion cried. "His cabin will be underwater. We have to leave now!"

"You go," Cass replied. "I have to at least try to save him."

"You are a soft-hearted fool, Goatsmilk! He is half-dead anyway!" Lion cried, but he did bend down over Kov's body and extract a loop of leather with some keys on it. "You had better take these," he said, throwing them at her.

Cass could hear Rip shouting as soon as she got below deck. She called out that she was coming but it wasn't easy – the ship had tilted so far to one side that half of it was underwater. She tied the keys on to the sash of her costume and tucked the dagger at the back so she could make her way along the corridor, swinging like a monkey from doorframe to doorframe. Luckily, Rip's cabin was on the higher side of the ship but even so, by the time she got there she was waist-deep in water, trying not to panic at the listing ship as she made her way along the dark corridor.

Rip had stopped shouting. *Please let him not be dead*, she prayed.

He wasn't, but he was standing as far away from the deep water as the chain would stretch, and his face was nearly submerged.

"What's going on!?" he spluttered.

"It's the Minarian Navy, come to rescue you," Cass replied, feeling behind Rip's back for the lock that was fastening his chain.

"Why are they trying to drown me then?" he asked.

Despite everything, Cass burst out laughing, as she began to try to fit each key in turn into the lock. It wasn't easy, and her hands kept fumbling with them. Twice she dropped the ring and had to duck down into the water to get it.

"I'm not wishing to rush you," Rip said. "But I think I need to point out that the water is about to cover my nose and mouth."

"I'm sorry," Cass cried, trying to fit another key

into the lock. *It's the wrong one*, she panicked as it refused to turn one way. And then as she turned it the other way, the lock gave a lurch and opened.

"Oh, thank goodness!" she said, as Rip shook off the chains. Cass helped him, and together they swam through the water, back up the corridors and out on to the deck, just as the boat gave another downward lurch.

"Come on!" Lion shouted, as they got out on deck, which was now so slanted they could hardly stand up straight. Cass could see that the deck of the other boat was still a scene of furious fighting and to her alarm, it looked as if the pirates might be winning.

"We will have to swim to shore," she announced.

"Not so fast," a voice said. And they all spun round to see Varen calmly standing at the other end of the deck, a sword in each hand. Before any of them could answer, he walked towards them and threw a sword at Rip, who caught it and the fight began.

Rip never really stood a chance. Cass could see what an excellent swordsman Varen was and before she could do anything, he had knocked the sword out of Rip's hand and plunged his blade into the boy's stomach. Rip screamed in agony and, his knees folding, fell to the ground in a heap.

"No!" screamed Cass, her emotions condensed to a single point of rage that came from deep inside her. She grabbed the sword that Rip had dropped.

Varen burst out laughing. "Are you sure, little girl, that you want to fight me?" he mocked.

"Why not?" Cass said. "You're going to kill me anyway."

"It's true," Varen replied and raised his sword. Cass crossed it with hers and they began.

Varen so underestimated Cass that she nearly had him. But he just managed to push her sword away in time and she only nicked his cheek, drawing a few drops of blood.

"You're actually rather good at this," Varen admitted. "I'd better start trying."

He came at Cass with all his strength, as if he were fighting a man and Cass had to use every bit of her wit and skill to keep her balance on the listing ship and ward off Varen's blows. She was close to getting him again, but then he started to swipe at her, forcing her back until she found herself jammed against the main mast. He put his weight against Cass, bending her sword arm back against herself.

"So at last it is done," he said.

"Just wait," Cass stalled, as she reached behind her back and extracted her dagger. "I have to tell you something," she said.

"What?" Varen asked, looking irritated.

"This," Cass replied, and shoved the dagger as hard as she could into his ribs. He cried out in surprise and fury, and shoved her across the deck with all his might. She fell heavily on her left hand and felt something snap in her wrist, but she was so intent on killing Varen that, ignoring the pain, she flung herself at Rip's sword. The pirate king was on his knees and without hesitation Cass plunged the sword into his heart.

There were shouts from nearby and Lion cried, "There's another boat coming! I think it's more pirates! Come on, we have to go!" He tugged at Cass's good hand. She looked down at the other, which was throbbing agonizingly. It was hanging at a strange angle and she knew immediately it was broken. The pain and the sight of it, along with everything else, was making her feel light-headed and sick.

"We must go!" Lion cried again, pulling at her.

"But what about Rip?" she said.

"He is dead. Please, we have to go now," he implored. "Please."

Cass knelt down by Rip. A great pool of blood had leaked out of his wound. There was no sign of life and when she tried to see if he was still breathing, she couldn't feel any movement in his chest. *Lion is right*, she thought. *He is dead or dying, and even if he is still alive, I cannot swim with him like this. I will barely be able to swim myself.*

As if he could read her thoughts, Lion said, "Cass, there is no choice! You must leave him now!"

Her eyes blurring with tears, she allowed Lion to drag her to the edge of the boat and jump into the water. They swam together to the shore, Cass using only one of her arms. Her wrist was agony. By the time they had hauled themselves up on to the beach, she looked back to see lights on the sinking ship. *Please let it be the Navy and not the pirates*, she prayed. *Please let them save Rip, please.* And then, despite the pain she was in, she fell into an exhausted sleep, there on the hard shingle.

The daylight and the agony of her wrist woke Cass a few hours later. She looked out to sea but there was nothing but the hull of *The Narina* poking out. There was no sign of the other pirate ship or the Navy. Whoever had been, had gone.

Feeling entirely numb with shock, Cass woke Lion and he helped her make a sling for her wrist out of his shirt. Then they got up, stiff, sore and thirsty, and walked the mile or so back to Sedoor. Attracting curious looks in their filthy, bloody clothes, they walked along the harbour only to find that the Circus Boat had left.

Cass would have sat down on the harbour wall and cried, had it not been for a familiar voice saying, "Cassandra, what in the Longest World has happened to you?" and the friendly, concerned face of Captain Bemot appearing. He ushered them on to his boat where he gave them each a tot of Rimple's Finest and listened to Cass's rearranged tale of the previous night, of how they had got caught up in a battle between the pirates and the Minarian Navy. For Cass and Lion had made the very sensible decision on the walk back to Sedoor that they would tell no one they had killed Kov and Varen. The pirates had many friends who would be sure to come looking for whoever had killed them. It was to be their secret.

"Why, then you must come back with me to Minaris, Cass, and you too, young man, if you so wish," the kind captain said.

With a sense of enormous relief, Cass agreed for herself.

"But Lion, don't you want to go home?" she asked.

"No," Lion replied, with the same hard look that Cass had seen him give on the boat. "There is nothing left there for me. Can I come with you?"

"Of course," she replied, without hesitation. She was sure Lin would have Lion to stay if Mrs Potts made a fuss.

The boat sailed later that day after Captain Bemot had taken Cass to an apothecary. The doctor had carefully examined her wrist and confirmed that she had indeed broken it, and badly. He gave Cass a large glass of island hooch, then set it before bandaging it up in a proper sling.

After *The Joyful Endeavour* set sail, Cass was braced for further disasters but the journey proved uneventful. They sailed a different route to the Circus Boat so there was no sign of them, although Cass's thoughts often wandered to Sofia. She presumed that Mercer had been killed by the explosion and she wondered if news of his death had reached his sister.

Cass wrote to Elsba again care of the Postage Office in Hendra, in a suitably cryptic way, in case the letter was intercepted and she sent a bird to Lady Sigh, saying that there had been a change in circumstances and she was on her way back to Minaris on a merchant's ship. At every port they stopped, the quays were alive with the news of the deaths of Varen and Kov, and also of Enzo, Cass learned with some sadness. His body had been washed up in Sedoor a few days after they left and Cass guessed that he too must have been killed by the explosion.

But of Rip she could find out nothing. She feared the worst but could not quite accept it until she heard definitely that he was dead. When they made a brief stop in Liversus, Cass finally saw a news sheet for sale. She practically tore it out of the vendor's hand, throwing coins at him. From it she learned that Enzo's body had been taken to his mother, where a simple funeral was held. And, blinking back tears of relief, Cass read that his cousin Rip had been rescued by Lycus's men, and was being nursed on Hospital Island where he remained dangerously ill.

About a week before they landed in Minaris, Cass woke up and realized it was her birthday. They docked at Loutrekia and Cass celebrated her fifteenth birthday and her coming of age quietly with Lion over cloud cakes and flower beer in a quayside inn.

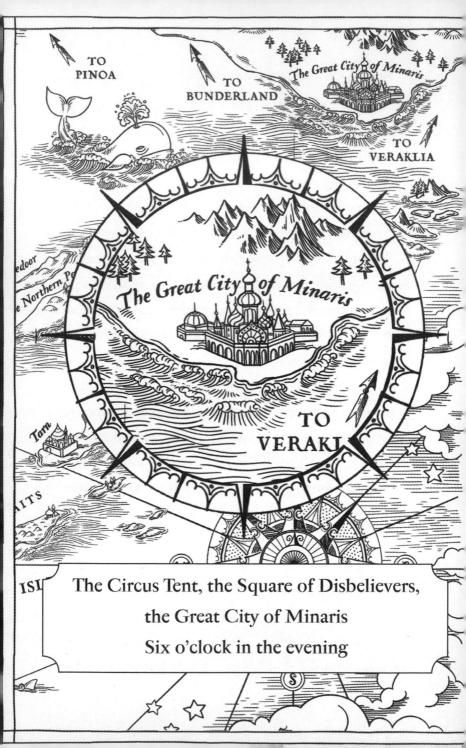

The Circus Tent, the Square of Disbelievers,
the Great City of Minaris
Six o'clock in the evening

XVIII

The Social Secretary

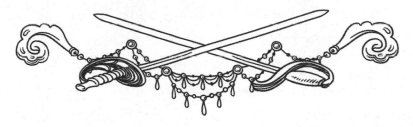

They arrived in Minaris in the middle of a snowstorm. But nothing could dampen Lion's spirits as he stood on deck looking like a small bear in the furs that Cass had bought him on the journey, thanks to a loan from Captain Bemot.

"I cannot believe such a city exists! It is as if it were built by giants!" he cried, gawping at what little he could see of the Great Lighthouse and the Seventy-Seven White Towers rising up like a forest in front of him.

Cass stood beside him as the boat docked on the Quay of Thieves, inhaling the familiar smell of wood smoke and clean cold. It felt good to be home, she decided.

Cass and Lion said a brief goodbye to Captain Bemot, promising to come and see him soon, and then, hoiking the little luggage that she had over her shoulder, Cass strapped on her own and Lion's newly purchased skates. She skated with him in front of her, holding him firmly under his arms, as she had grown up seeing Minarian mothers doing with their children. As they weaved their way along the streets towards the Square of Seas and the snow was still gently falling in great flakes, Lion shrieked with excitement.

To say Mrs Potts was surprised to see Cass would be an understatement. Cass had meant to write to her, but somehow she had never got around to it. So when poor Mrs Potts opened the door to them, the sight of Cass had made her faint with shock, and it took several large sniffs of her smelling salts, three cups of bitter tea liberally laced with Rimple's and a long lie-down on the sofa to restore her to health. Meanwhile, Cass and Lion sat with Tig in the kitchen, drinking hot cacao, eating Tig's delicious floury drop cakes and swapping tales of their adventures with the news of the square. The fortune teller who had so charmed Mrs Potts had turned out to be a thief as well as a lousy fortune teller, and he had run off in the middle of the night with several pieces of Mrs Potts's jewellery as well as owing several weeks' rent.

"So you can have your old room back," Tig said.

"Please can we go out in the snow again," Lion said, looking longingly out of the window. The storm had passed and the sun had come out, making everything look sparkling and magical.

"You go and play in the square," Cass said. "I'm going to see Lin."

"Cass! Come in," Lin said, her strange green-blue eyes shining. She took both Cass's hands in hers.

"Thank you for saving me from drowning," Cass found herself blurting out. "I would never have made it to the Island of Women without you."

Lin smiled and said, "It was just luck – I was trancing and saw you, and I could help. I'm sorry

I couldn't come to your aid later on but it sounds as if you did a good job on your own. Dear Cass, you have had such a time," she went on. "And you have come home all grown up. How do you feel now?"

Cass hesitated before saying, "I know I should feel happy because everything is over and we are safe. But somehow I feel flat, as if I were a balloon that someone has let too much air out of."

Lin smiled. "I can see you have lost some of your lightness – but it will return, don't worry. Do you know what you will do? Will you continue with the Circus?"

"I'm not sure," Cass replied. She flexed her left wrist, which was out of the sling but still felt sore and weak. "I broke my wrist and it doesn't seem to be healing properly."

"Then you must go and see this apothecary. It may be that it needs re-setting," Lin said, scribbling an address on a piece of paper. "Doctor Andreas is the best bone doctor in Minaris." And then Lin excused herself as she had to see a client.

Doctor Andreas examined Cass's wrist gently and after a few moments she said, "That was a bad break. You're lucky it wasn't your writing hand." She paused, making Cass nervous. "But it has mended well enough. Now you need to exercise it. Every day like this, and like this." She showed her several moves.

"And will it recover entirely?" Cass asked hopefully. "I am an acrobat – will it bear my weight again?"

The apothecary paused and then shook her head sadly, "No, I don't think so. It should recover enough for everyday use, but not for that, I'm afraid."

Trying not to cry, Cass thanked her and made her way back home. She ran into Tig on the stairs, who was kind, saying, "Perhaps Ravellous can devise an act for you using only your good arm? Or maybe there's something else you can do with the Circus? Why don't you speak to him? The Circus Boat is due to arrive in a couple of weeks – I saw the posters yesterday."

Cass sighed and said she would. She woke up the next morning and, trying to feel hopeful, decided that perhaps Dr Andreas was wrong. So she did her exercises religiously, and after about a week, her wrist did seem much better and it no longer pained her to hold a bag or wash the dishes. But whenever she tentatively put weight on it, she could feel how weak it was. The day of the Circus Boat's arrival came and went, and although she knew she should go and see Ravellous, she couldn't face it, and every day she found a reason to postpone it.

As the last of winter receded, Cass spent her days taking long skates around the city on the increasingly mushy ice, wondering what she should do with her life and trying not to think constantly about Rip. She had several letters from Annabella, full of funny drawings and long descriptions of Von and all her other creatures, and a couple of shorter notes from Lady Sigh and Pela. Perhaps she should return to the Island of Women, Cass wondered. But something about that choice didn't feel right. A short letter also arrived from Elsba, which alluded to Cass killing Varen and praising her for her bravery. She signed it off saying that she was on her way to Minaris and looked forward to seeing Cass soon. Perhaps she would help with her decision, Cass hoped.

And Lion? Well, it had been, Cass reflected later, love at second or even third sight, between Lion and Mrs Potts. After the old lady's shock at seeing Cass had subsided, Lion had caught her eye. For the first day she had been unsure of him, but then his charm had begun to work its magic. By the end of the second day, particularly when she saw how useful he could be with the clients, she pronounced him a "dear little chap". The following day Mrs Potts took him clothes shopping, and much to Cass and Tig's amusement, brought him home dressed up like a Minarian merchant's son and announced her intention in enrolling him in Mrs Papworth's Academy to learn his letters and sums. And Lion seemed absolutely delighted by it all.

Much to Cass's relief, the issue with Ravellous ending up resolving itself. She sent him a note saying that she was back in Minaris and could she see him? He appeared the following day, clutching a large bunch of flowers, and Cass's trunk was plonked down on the doorstep by a couple of circusters. Ravellous made a great fuss of Cass and Mrs Potts, who decided that perhaps Circus people were not so bad after all, and he generally behaved as if Cass and he had got separated at a party, rather than him leaving her stranded in Sedoor after nearly being killed by pirates.

He listened attentively as she told him about her wrist and then said in his serious tone,

"Cass, after that night, there will always be a place for you with the Circus. If you cannot work as an acrobat, you could learn some clowning perhaps? Female clowns are rare and it could be a draw…"

Cass tried to imagine herself clowning, but the image wouldn't conjure itself. However, she thanked him for the offer and promised to consider it.

"How is Sofia?" she asked as he was about to leave.

"Transformed," he replied. "She was sad at first obviously but now it's as if she can breathe finally."

"I don't understand," Cass replied, frowning.

"What do you mean?"

"Her brother's death released her somehow. You would hardly recognize her – she is as chatty as Bassa and twice as mischievous."

Ravellous left with Cass promising to come and see them all soon.

The week of the royal wedding arrived and the whole city was in high spirits. The ice had melted and the last of the Spring Equinox floods had washed the city clean. The normally riotous Feast of the Receding Tide was a little calmer than usual as Minarians devoted themselves to decorating the streets for the wedding. Miles and miles of thick red ribbon was crisscrossed high above the narrow streets, and hundreds of boxes of red flower petals were handed out to everyone to shower the bridal party. Then the parties inevitably began, and the merchants' houses were lit up until the early hours, while the inns overflowed into the streets as the city drank to the health and happiness of King Lycus and his fiancée, the Pinoan Princess Arden.

The day of the princess's arrival came. Mrs Potts had a friend who lived in a house on the route that the royal party was to take, so Cass and she stood with others on the first-floor balcony, and threw handfuls of petals over Princess Arden and her family as their sledges glided slowly by. *She's so young, hardly older than me*, Cass thought, catching her first glimpses of Arden. And then she gave a jump of recognition as sitting next to the princess, her red hair glinting like fire, was Idaliz. Her breeches and waistcoat were gone and she was dressed as a lady-in-waiting. *So that had been her business in Pinoa*, Cass thought with amusement, *guarding the Princess Arden*. At that moment, Idaliz looked up and seeing Cass, smiled and winked.

It was the following day that the boy brought the letter. It was addressed to Cass and as she didn't recognize the writing, she wondered whether it was from Rip. She tore open the envelope, sending a card fluttering to the floor. It was black on one side with a white eight in the middle of it, and on the other side was written, in a neat calligraphic hand,

*You are invited to a meeting at
the Inn of the Garbled Nightingale,
the Port of Many Possibilities, at six this evening.*

Cass felt a jolt of excitement.

The inn was a very old, higgledy-piggledy building, tucked away at the far end of the port. Cass walked into the main room, which was crowded with sailors. There was no sign of Elsba or any other women and Cass was about to ask the landlord when she saw a board that read, *Meeting Tonight of the Genteel Ladies of Astrology with Guest Speaker, Dr Regus*, and an arrow pointing up a rickety old staircase.

Cass knocked tentatively on the door and was delighted when it was thrown open by Elsba, who had transformed herself yet again – this time into a highly respectable-looking Minarian lady, dressed like Lady Sigh in a copper-coloured silk dress, with her hair braids piled intricately on top of her head.

"Cass! I am so glad to see you!" she cried, hugging her.

"Hello, Cass," another voice said and Idaliz came forward, dressed similarly. "I hope you are very proud of yourself," she said. "I still cannot believe what you did. Quite amazing. And here are some other people who are very keen to meet you."

Feeling slightly self-conscious, Cass followed Elsba and Idaliz to a group of four other women.

"Cass, please can I introduce you to some other members of the Company – this is Lai and Niv, who were in the Far Isles. And this is Ada, who was with me in the Mid Isles. It was Ada who was alerted by one of our friends in Sedoor about your note and sent the Navy to you."

"Thank you," Cass said to Ada.

"It is an honour to meet you, Cass," Ada said. "We all have so much to thank you for, ridding the Longest World of Varen and Kov."

Cass mumbled something about just being lucky, but Lai interrupted her. "Nonsense! That was not about luck, Cass. It was about exceptional courage and a very talented sword arm."

"I am only sorry that we could not get to you

ourselves in time to help," Elsba said.

"I'm not sure Cass needed our help!" Niv said with a laugh. "You should be very proud of yourself."

"You certainly should," a voice said as the door opened to reveal a man. It was difficult to see his face he was so swathed in a large cloak and hood.

"Ah, our guest speaker, Dr Rebus," Niv said, sounding amused, and then to Cass's surprise, she made a low bow to him, as did the others. Cass was mystified until he threw back his hood and to her amazement she saw that the man was none other than King Lycus. She dropped into a low curtsy, as taught to her in etiquette lessons at Mrs Papworth's Academy.

"It is I who should be bowing to you, Cass," he said, taking her hand and helping her up. "What a thing you did!"

Lai handed around glasses of winter wine and everyone toasted Cass.

"So, Elsba tells me you are an acrobat," Lycus said to Cass. "Is that what you will do now? Rejoin the Circus?" he asked.

"Perhaps," Cass replied unsurely. "I broke my

wrist, when I was..." she hesitated to speak of Varen. "That night ... and it has mended but not well enough to be an acrobat again, so now I am not sure what to do."

"I'm sorry," Lycus replied. "That must be devastating for you."

Cass nodded. "I really loved it. And now I have to find something else to do," she said.

There was a pause before Elsba said, "Well, I have an idea. Perhaps you might like to come to the Islands with us." She gestured to the other women. "The king has asked us to accompany Rip, who is to return there next month to try to restore order there and capture the remaining pirates. You would be invaluable to us in identifying them, not to mention using your incredible fighting skills."

Cass was surprised but also to her alarm, felt herself blush slightly at Rip's name. *Oh, pull yourself together*, she told herself sternly.

Lycus continued, explaining to Cass, "There is also still one of Varen's lieutenants at large and I am concerned that he will take charge."

Unable to resist the temptation to talk about Rip, Cass asked, "So is he much better? R-Rip, I mean." She felt herself stutter slightly, annoying herself even more.

"His wounds have almost healed, but he is still quite weak. I hope he will be well enough to return to Minaris for my wedding," Lycus replied.

"So what do you think, Cass?" Idaliz asked. "Will you come and help us?"

An adventure to the Far Isles with Rip and Elsba, and a chance to bring the pirates to justice. Cass couldn't think of anything she would like more, yet she found herself throwing obstacles in the way.

"No, I can't come," she said hurriedly. "It is not fair on Mrs Potts, my guardian. She would have a fit – being an acrobat was bad enough, but fighting pirates would finish her off, and I caused her so much anxiety when I ran away. She is elderly and it is not good for her to worry. "

"She need never know. In fact, it is better and safer if she doesn't," Lycus pointed out. "We can think of something suitable to tell her."

"But is it what you want, Cass? To come with us?" Ada asked.

Cass thought. She knew Minaris would always

be home, but there was so much more she wanted to do, to see in the world. She had loved being part of a group, both on the Palace Ship initially and on the Circus Boat. And she wanted to help the Company, especially if it meant finally stopping the pirates. So she took a deep breath.

"Yes," she said. "I would love to come."

The women cheered and Lycus said, "Excellent. Now I must get back to the palace, but I hope that you will come to the wedding? And do you think your guardian would like to come too?"

Cass had to stop herself bursting into laughter at the thought of Mrs Potts's reaction to going to the royal wedding.

"Yes, thank you, sire, I rather think she would," she replied.

As Cass had predicted, Mrs Potts's shrieks of excitement when a liveried footman arrived on her doorstep bearing a royal invitation, reverberated around the Square of Seas like pistol shots. The noise brought all the neighbours to their doors, concerned that someone was being murdered.

"Oh, I am sorry," she called to them, secretly delighted that they had all seen the footman. "Just a little note from the palace. It took me quite by surprise."

The wedding was only a couple of days away and this sent Mrs Potts into a whirl of activity, much of which was directed at making Cass "look respectable". Cass submitted good-naturedly to the old lady's desires, visiting Mr Magenta who got rid of the last brown tinges to her hair and cut the tangles from the bottom. There was no time to have a dress made but after a bit of rootling around at Parker's Emporium, Cass found a silver dress that she loved and even Mrs Potts pronounced "most becoming".

The wedding party started at midday, and the whole square turned out to see Mrs Potts and Cass off. Mrs Potts had outdone herself in a purple velvet ensemble, with a matching rinse in her hair, but everyone told her she looked very nice.

"You look like a princess," Lion said approvingly to Cass as he examined her in the silver dress. "So much better than normal."

Since there was such a jam of carriages and crowds around the palace, it had been decided that Mrs Potts would travel in a sedan chair and Cass would walk. Cass, who had woken at dawn, her stomach fluttering at the thought of seeing Rip, welcomed the opportunity to be out on her own in the warm spring sunshine. She saw the old lady safely off and was about to leave herself, when Lin appeared.

"Cass, you look lovely and you know what, you have..."

"Don't say it!" Cass cried, but with a laugh. "The star you saw over my head brought me no luck last time."

"But perhaps it will today," Lin replied with a smile.

The great halls of the palace were crowded with brilliantly dressed guests. Mrs Potts was exclaiming rapturously over the trays of wine and food that were being brought round, and she kept up a steady stream of chat about all the faces that she recognized from the gossip sheets. As Cass nervously scanned the crowds she tried to tell herself it was to see if there was anyone she knew, though really she was only looking for one person.

Mrs Potts was insistent that they should make their way through the crowds to congratulate the "royal couple". As they came into the Great Hall, Cass saw Rip standing a little way off, on the stairs, talking to Ornella. After thinking about him so much, it was such a shock to see him that Cass felt as if she had conjured him up. Ornella saw Cass and whispered something to Rip, who looked at her too and smiled. Feeling herself going crimson, Cass looked away and pretended to be very interested in her drink.

"You do look hot, Cassandra dear! Are you feeling faint? Come and stand by the window here," Mrs Potts said, pulling her over to an open window and fanning her just as Rip and Ornella appeared. Cass thought she would die of embarrassment but then the strangest thing happened. As they all introduced each other, and Mrs Potts simpered with pleasure at meeting them, Rip quietly and calmly slipped his hand into hers, as if it were the most natural thing in the world, and she felt all her awkwardness float away up into the air, up to the painted ceilings and beyond, and a smile grew and grew on her face, until she feared she would be nothing but smile. There seemed so much to say to him about Enzo and Bastien, and that terrible night with Varen, but she knew they could talk about it later, when they were alone. So they just stood silently for a moment as Ornella told Mrs Potts about her recent engagement, and Mrs Potts made all the right noises. Then Ornella excused herself.

"What a lovely young woman!" Mrs Potts sighed. "So beautiful and gracious! I hope that young Pinoan Count knows how lucky he is!"

Rip smiled. "I think he does – she reminds him often enough." And they all laughed.

"Mrs Potts," Rip began. "I wanted to ask if you'd be willing to let Cassandra come on a voyage to the Far Isles with me, as my social secretary. As I'm sure you know, that was her job on my uncle's ship and she was so superb at it that I am really keen for her to come and help arrange all the parties and dinners that I will have to hold."

Cass suppressed a giggle while Mrs Potts hesitated.

"But would it be dangerous? I've heard talk of pirates in the Islands," she said. "I wouldn't want my Cassandra to be put in any danger."

"I'm sure it would be no worse than her trip to the Island of Women," Rip replied truthfully.

"Well, that went smoothly enough, didn't it?" Mrs Potts said. "You know, it doesn't surprise me that she has such a knack for social matters. I have always brought her up to know how important such things are, and I was quite the girl about town in my youth." She patted her purple curls. "Yes, I could spare her, I think," she mused. "And to be a social secretary is so much nicer than an acrobat. Although I have to say that Mr Ravellous was a most charming man." She turned to Cass. "Would you like to go, dear?"

"I would," Cass replied.

"Oh, very well. Then of course you may. And with my blessing."

Rip thanked Mrs Potts as Cass glanced out of the window beside her. It looked over the Great Quay and she smiled to see the Circus Boat moored there, its jaunty bunting dancing in the breeze. But then her eye was drawn beyond the boat, out to the vast expanse of blue-grey sea and the Islands that she knew lay out there. And she felt a delicious feeling of excitement and anticipation at the thought of all the adventures to come, with Rip and the Company of Eight.

Acknowledgements

I need to say a huge thank you to my brilliant agent, Catherine Pellegrino, for her unwavering support and generally being great. And also to everyone at Stripes who have worked so hard on the book and have been such a pleasure to work with.

Particular thanks go to
Ruth Bennett and Rachel Boden for
their masterful editing, Charlie Morris for
her excellent marketing campaign,
Pip Johnson in the art department for
making the book look brilliant and to the
artist Maria Surducan for her
amazing cover.

Harriet Whitehorn grew up in London,
where she still lives with her husband and three
daughters. She studied at Reading University
and the Architectural Association, and previously
worked in building conservation. She is now a
full-time writer and has also written the Violet
series, which is published by Simon and Schuster.

Although she is not known for her fondness
for boats or acrobatic skills, nevertheless,
there's a part of her that would have loved
to run away on a Circus Boat.